Also by Michelle Gordon:

Earth Angel Series:
The Earth Angel Training Academy
The Earth Angel Awakening
The Other Side

Visionary Collection:
Heaven dot com
The Doorway to PAM
The Elphite
I'm Here

Oracle Cards:
Aria's Oracle
Velvet's Oracle
Amethyst's Oracle

The Twin Flame Reunion

Michelle Gordon

theamethystangel.com

First published in Great Britain in 2014 by The Amethyst Angel

Copyright © 2014 by Michelle Gordon
Cover illustration by Jason Mordecai & Michelle Gordon
Copyright © The Amethyst Angel

ISBN: 978-1502932501

First Edition

Gratitude

There is a core group of people that I express my gratitude for in the creation of every book I have published. This time, instead of simply writing something, I have decided to do something a little different. You can see my gratitude for those amazing people on my blog at twinflameblog.com/gratitude.

There are many other people who have been there along the way, so I would like to thank them here.

Love to my beautiful Spiritual Sisters, Anne, Kelly, Buckso and Lisa. We will all meet up again soon, I promise.

So much love and hugs to all my amazing Earth Angel friends who have helped me through the last year, and with the creation of this book: Niki and Dan, Lucja Fratczak-Kay, Sarah Vine, Loubie Lou, Hannah Imogen Jones, Angela Raasch, Louise Sophia Weir, Rhys Westbury, Rachael Barnwell, Miranda Adams, Lana Feeney, Ray Ball, Roxanne Barker, Tiffany Hathorn, Janina Irvin, Lisa Jones, Liz Chukwu and Keith Bound.

So much love and gratitude to my Brighton family, Chip, Joni, Zula, Chas, Mike, Alan, Tim, Heather, Paul, Annan, Klare, Kush, Bill, Annie, Lily; thank you all for making me feel welcome and at home in this vibrant city.

A huge bundle of gratitude for my beautiful readers and fans who keep me writing, particularly: Helen Gordon, Richard Grey, Annette Ecuyere, Rosa Lewis, Wenna Macormac, Paul Killen, Cyndi Sabido, Llinos Thomas, Janet Spillane Gupwell, Lisa Fuqua, Robyn Peters, Emerald and Xander.

And finally, Jimmy, I am so glad that you have a smile on your face and a song in your heart again. You are an inspiration, thank you.

This book is dedicated to all Twin Flames.
Love each other unconditionally, and never give up,
even if you have to let go.

Chapter One

"Greg!"

Violet and Greg pulled away from each other to see Amy stood in the doorway. Greg smiled and pulled Violet close to his side, not wanting to let her go.

"Amy, it's good to see you."

Amy came over to them, looking like she was unsure whether to hug him or slap him. "How come you're here? How did you know where we were?"

"Leona gave me your parents' address, and then your mum told me you were here. I had to see Violet," he looked down at his Flame. "I had an Awakening of sorts. I realised what would happen if we were to stay apart," his voice faltered, and he didn't bother wiping away the tear making its way down his cheek. He looked back up at Amy, whose expression was more compassionate than confused now. "As soon as I realised, I got in the van and drove back to the UK."

Amy looked at Violet, who was smiling widely, and smiled in return. She reached out and hugged them both. "I'm so glad you finally came to your senses," she muttered into Greg's ear. He chuckled and nodded.

"Me too."

Amy pulled back, shaking her head. "Something weird happened during the meditation, we all experienced it."

Violet frowned. "What do you mean?"

"We all had visions of our lives, spanning two decades, then the feeling of being outside of our bodies, and on the Other Side. Then we all felt something like an electric shock, like we had re-entered our bodies again."

Violet raised her eyebrows. "That is weird. I wonder what that was about. What happened in the visions?"

Amy frowned, the memory of hers was hazy already. "It's a bit blurry now, but I'm pretty sure I met Nick."

"Nick?" Greg asked.

"Amy's Twin Flame. His name came up in the meditation we did the first time we were here," Violet explained. "What did the others see? Are they still outside?"

Amy nodded. "They wanted to rest after the weird shock, but Esmeralda said you had come in and I wanted to make sure you were okay."

"Thank you." Violet looked up at Greg. "I'm very okay now."

Amy laughed. "I can see that. I think they'll all be in for a cuppa and some cake in a minute, so I'll go and put the kettle on." She reached out and squeezed Greg's arm. "It is good to see you again."

"You too," Greg said.

Amy went to the kitchen, and Violet and Greg listened to the sound of the tap and the clinking of mugs for a few seconds. Then they both started to speak at once.

Laughing, Greg gestured for Violet to go first.

"I was just going to ask, what happens now?"

"I assume we will have a cuppa and I will have a bit of explaining to do to the rest of your friends."

Violet shook her head. "No, I mean with us. Have you decided what it is you want? Only I don't think I can go through losing you again."

Greg held her tighter, and pain flitted across his face. "I will be completely honest – I haven't thought it all out yet. All I knew was I had to get here as soon as I could, in case anything happened to you."

The memory of the icy cold water slipping over her head suddenly made Violet gasp. "How did you know?"

"Know what?"

Violet shook her head. "Never mind."

Just then, Esmeralda, Mike, Maggie, Beattie, Keeley, Leila and Fay all came into the house. There were several gasps of shock and delight when they saw Violet and Greg standing by the piano. Greg wanted to question Violet on what she had meant, but that intention slipped away as he tried to explain to her friends why he had suddenly come to his senses, and realised how much he loved Violet.

*   *   *

They had waited until all who wanted to return had left, and then had chosen whose lives and bodies they wanted to walk into. They hoped that their choice would ensure they would meet again once they got to Earth.

"What if we don't find each other?" Aria whispered, as she stared into the white mists.

"Don't be silly, of course we will," Linen responded, his hand tightening around hers. "I will make sure of it." They turned to each other and kissed for a long time, until Gold had to clear his throat and snap them out of it.

Aria looked over her shoulder and smiled at him. "Sorry! See you again soon."

Gold smiled, but his right eye twitched as he replied. "I look forward to it."

Without any further hesitation, Linen and Aria flew into the mists, not letting go of each other's hands until the last moment.

*   *   *

"Anna! It's time to get up! You're going to be late! Again!"

Her eyes flew open upon hearing the exclamations and she looked around the unfamiliar room. Where the hell was she? She tried to move, but her limbs felt like they weighed a million pounds.

"Help!" she called out, then her eyes widened at the sound of her own voice. It didn't sound like her at all. "Help?" she said again, as she put more effort into moving her body. "Linen?" she called out without thinking.

Suddenly, a thousand memories slammed through her mind at top speed, leaving her panting for breath. "Oh my God!" she squeaked. "I'm human!" She lifted her hand up; it looked like a giant's hand. Her eyes widened, and she sat up suddenly. She reached behind her and felt between her shoulder blades. "My wings!" she cried. Still breathing heavily, Aria turned to see the door to the room opening, and an unfamiliar woman stepped in.

"Anna!" the woman said. "I'm serious, if you don't get going right now, you're going to get sacked. I am not calling them and pretending you're ill again."

Eyes wide, she stared at the woman, knowing that she should recognise her somehow, but not having a clue of her identity. "Who are you?" she asked.

The woman looked at her incredulously. "Amnesia? Oh, now that is a whole new low for you. Faking headaches and stomach-aches is one thing, but stop being ridiculous. Get up and get ready for work. I am not coming up here again. If you get sacked it will be your own fault." She left the room muttering, "No idea why they would hire you in the first place."

Feeling close to tears at the harsh words of the strange woman, Aria somehow managed to get her incredibly heavy body out of the bed and over to the mirror in the corner of the room. Her eyes widened when she took in her reflection. Straggly hair, skinny limbs (so why on earth did she feel so heavy?) and big green eyes. Pleased that she actually looked like her old Faerie self, another realisation suddenly hit her.

"Oh my goodness! I remembered!" she exclaimed, not caring if the nasty woman heard her. A big grin spread across her face. All the worry she'd had about forgetting who she was, about forgetting her friends and those she loved, was all for nothing. She remembered everything. She dashed across the room to the desk to find some paper and a pen, scared suddenly that although she could remember now, she might forget again soon.

In her rummage through the big messy pile of papers and assorted junk on the desk, she found a small black object, and recognised it as being a video camera, from all the times she had watched humans on Earth. Perhaps she could record her memories instead?

Not wanting to stick around in case the nasty lady came back, Aria put the camera in what looked like a handbag, and then grabbed some clothing from the floor and clumsily got dressed. She shoved her feet into a pair of ballet-style shoes and left the room, checking the hallway was clear before making her way out of the house. She got lost a couple of times on the way out, and marvelled at the fact that she was still very much the same easily confused, clumsy Faerie.

She found the front door and was about to exit the house when she heard someone behind her.

"If you go dressed like that, you'll definitely get sacked! And if you think I'm going to pay for your food and clothes, you've got another thing coming!"

Without turning around to acknowledge the nasty lady, she slipped through the door and ran down the path. It was colder than she had anticipated, and her feet felt like they were made of lead. The camera in the bag thumped against her leg, making her wish she could fly again. When she was sure that the lady wasn't following her, she slowed down a little and tried to catch her breath. She started to take in her surroundings, and couldn't help but feel complete awe. The last time she had been on Earth, she had been in the Elemental Realm, and was a tiny Faerie who was smaller than a blade of grass. As she adjusted to her new body, she got used to her weight and density, and began to enjoy the walk. She recalled the moment when all of her classmates at the Academy had received a human body, and how they had told her how heavy it was, and how she had freaked out and refused to become human.

She chuckled to herself at the memory, startling a bird perched on a bare tree branch. She watched it fly away and sighed. As much as she tried to quash it, a strong feeling of jealousy washed over her.

She had chosen this. She recalled the moment she had decided to come back as a human. It seemed like such a crazy idea now, why had she wanted to experience this?

Just then, as if in answer to her musings, a flying ladybug zoomed over and landed on her arm. She stopped in shock and stared at it, amazed at how absolutely tiny it was. She thought of Larry, and couldn't believe that she had once been small enough to be his best friend.

"Larry?" she whispered to the tiny insect. "Is that you?" The ladybug took flight again, and she followed it across the grass, until she found a beautiful spot in the middle of a circle of trees, far away from the main street she had been walking down. She lost sight of the ladybug, but decided this would be the perfect spot to record her memories, before they slipped away.

She found a branch at the right height to hold the camera, and then sat on the grass in front of it. She ignored the cold dampness seeping into her clothes and silently stared at the red light for a few moments before beginning to speak.

"My name is Aria, and I am a Faerie," she began, relaxing as the words flowed. "I have come to this planet from the Other Side, where I was first a trainee at the Earth Angel

Training Academy, then assistant head of the School for the Children of the Golden Age, and then the head of the Academy for Awakened Humans."

*　　*　　*

He was stalking his prey, sneaking down a back street, gun in hand. Breathing heavily, he slithered forward, knowing that his enemy stood, unsuspecting, right around the corner. A second later, he launched himself out into the main street, and pointed his gun at the man's head.

"Say hello to Satan for me," he drawled, before pulling the trigger.

"You know, that's really quite sadistic."

Charlie looked away from his digital self on the screen at the woman standing in the doorway of his bedroom. "Do I look like I care what you think?" he asked his mother sarcastically.

She sighed and closed the door, leaving him to stare at the dead body of his fallen enemy. Usually, it would have given him so much pleasure, but ever since he had split up from Violet, months before, he found it left him feeling quite hollow. He grabbed the remote and switched the TV off. Remembering the time when Violet had done the same thing in the middle of his game, and he had threatened her, he sighed. He threw the controller on the floor, disgusted with himself.

No wonder she had dumped him. He was pathetic. He got to his feet with the intention of showering and getting changed out of the clothes he had been wearing for the last three days, when suddenly he was assaulted by a stream of images in his mind. He saw himself learning of Violet's death, he saw himself spiralling out of control into darkness and despair, and he thought he glimpsed a beautiful woman, who wasn't Violet, but her eyes reminded him of her, but she was gone in a flash, and he remained alone until he died of cancer and a broken heart.

Gasping, Charlie clutched his chest, realising that in that moment he had fallen to the floor, and was laying amongst empty junk food cartons and dirty socks. He sat up and leaned back against the side of his bed. Then he did something that he never normally allowed himself to do.

He cried.

*   *   *

"My plan appears to be working then."

Gold looked up from the lake where he was watching the Earth Angels and he smiled at Starlight. "It would seem so, yes. I do wish you had enlightened me of all of this a little sooner though."

Starlight settled down beside him on the pebbly shore and sighed. "If I could have been absolutely certain of this outcome, believe me, I would have told you sooner. But it was still always possible that Velvet would choose to remain with me, among the stars, and not return to Earth."

"It was a risk, hoping that she would. I still think it would have been better to have just stopped her from leaving in the first place."

Starlight shook her head. "No it wouldn't. You see, even though you have turned back the clock, and you have given Earth another twenty years, all that happened in the time without Velvet is still retained within the soul of each Earth Angel. The ones who are open and Awake enough will remember. And the memories of that other time-line will change them. It will motivate them to live differently, and it is all these changes that will bring about the Golden Age."

Gold raised an eyebrow. "You cannot still believe that the Golden Age is a possibility? That Velvet will make things different enough this time? I thought the end of the current human civilisation was certain?"

Starlight laughed and placed her hand on his arm. "Just like you were certain that we would never have the chance to be together again?"

"What are you saying?" Gold whispered, his eyes locked on Starlight, a mixture of longing, confusion, love and fear entangled in his expression.

"I am saying, Gold, that if every soul on Earth has been given a second chance, if they have been given the opportunity to reunite with their Flames, then why should we not be given the same benefits?"

"Do you mean..."

"Yes, I mean that we will be together again, but," she sighed. "Not yet."

Gold frowned, his hopeful look gone. "When?"

"When I get back from Earth."

"Earth? You're going to Earth?" His expression tore at Starlight's heart.

"Yes, my dear love. I am going to Earth. It became clear to me, when spending all that time with Velvet, that she may need me again. And that I can help her. But not from my place in the stars. I need to be human, I need to stand beside her, and help her to take the world into the Golden Age."

Gold shook his head. "What do the Elders think?"

"It was their suggestion, actually. They felt there should be one of us on Earth at this time. So I volunteered to go."

Gold stared at the surface of the lake. "But that means I will not see you again for so long."

"Have I not said before? That this separation is but an illusion?" She took his hand and held it to her heart. "We are one. We are never apart. And as you know, time moves differently here than to Earth, it will merely feel like days or weeks to you." She leaned her head against his shoulder. "But to me, it will be a lifetime."

"How will you do it? As a walk-in?"

Starlight shook her head. "No, there would be too much of

a risk that I may not remember enough. I am just going to arrive on Earth, as myself, as Angels sometimes do."

"Just appear? What about your identity? How will you live?"

"Shh, my love," Starlight put her fingers to his lips. "You needn't worry about the details, for they will be taken care of."

Gold kissed her fingers, and then put his arm around her, avoiding her wings, which then encircled them both. "What will I do without you?" he whispered. "You are my guiding star, my shining light in the heavens. Who will look after everything and make sure it all runs smoothly?"

"You will do an excellent job of it, I wish you would have more faith in yourself. Besides, the Elders have promised to fill any gaps." She looked up at his profile, and her heart felt heavy at the look of sorrow etched on his face, and the lone tear making its way down his cheek. "When I get back, it will be our time. The Elders have agreed that because I have volunteered to do this, we can be together once again."

Gold closed his eyes. His heart filled with joy at the thought, yet felt heavy with pain at the idea of her being so far away from him.

"I will not be so far away," she whispered, placing her hand on his heart. "You will be within me, as I am within you, always."

He nodded, unable to speak. Starlight turned toward the lake, and they watched life on Earth for a while. After a few moments, she sighed.

"Must you go now?" he asked, afraid of the answer.

"Yes."

As one, they rose to their feet, and Gold stared into her eyes, trying to take in every last detail of his Twin Flame's beautiful face. "I love you, Starlight. And I wish you the very best with your mission. Please pass on my regards to Velvet and Laguz."

"I will. I love you, dear, sweet Gold. And I will see you

again soon." She reached up to kiss him, and tasted the saltiness of his tears.

She stepped away, and his arms fell to his sides. Before he could say another word, she disappeared in a swirl of tiny sparkling lights.

"Goodbye," he whispered.

*   *   *

After three days of hearing no news from Greg, or even Violet or Amy, Leona was getting bored of her own company. She fed the animals and then wrapped up warm, determined to go for a walk to get some air and hopefully bump into some locals she could practice her terrible French on.

Once outside, her hair whipped around in the wintry sea breeze, and she instantly began to feel better. She considered taking her shoes off to walk right along the water's edge, but then shivered. It would be silly to get too cold and become ill. Especially if Greg wasn't planning on returning anytime soon. She paused for a moment to pick up a shell, and when she bent over, she was suddenly immersed in a vision.

It was more realistic than her usual visions, and within seconds, she felt like she had lived through twenty years. When the images disappeared, she blinked rapidly, staring down at the shell in her hand, wondering what on earth had just happened. Out of everything she had just seen, the most vivid part was the face of her Twin Flame. Leona stood motionless on the sand, staring out to sea, but only seeing the long red hair, bright blue eyes and wide smile.

In just a matter of moments, Leona's whole world had changed. And everything now made sense. She tried to recall more details of her Flame, but all she could remember was being in a city. She closed her eyes and concentrated on picturing something, anything that would give her a clue as to where the city was. But she couldn't see past that beautiful smile. Sighing in frustration, Leona opened her eyes. She looked down at the seashell, and decided she would keep it until she found her Flame. It would be her talisman, her reminder of the vision. If she held onto it, she would hopefully find the one who made her heart race, who fitted perfectly in her embrace, who was the other half of her soul.

Chapter Two

"I still cannot believe you came to find me," Violet whispered, as she stroked Greg's face. "It feels like a dream, and that I might wake up at any moment."

"It's not a dream. It's real, I promise. And I won't leave your side again." He smiled. "I'm just so thankful you forgave me for all I did and said, and that you have allowed me back into your heart again."

Violet was quiet for a while. She looked around the dimly lit pod, where they had decided to stay for a few days, and she tried to find the right words. "I decided it wasn't worth holding onto the bad things," she whispered finally, turning her gaze back to him. "A couple of weeks ago, I went for a walk along the beach," she winced internally at her slight omission of the truth. "And suddenly, the weight in my chest, the sorrow of losing you, lifted. I felt lighter again. But I must admit, up until that moment, I had been in a very dark place."

Greg nodded. "Me too. I replayed that morning over and over again, hating myself for what I said, for how I made you feel. I realise now that it wasn't that I didn't love you, it was that I was afraid."

Violet frowned. "Afraid of what?"

"Of losing you."

"But that makes no sense," Violet said. "If you were so

afraid of losing me, why did you push me away?"

Greg sighed and rolled onto his back, staring up at the curved wooden ceiling. "I know it makes no sense, and to be honest, throughout the whole drive here, I tried to come up with a logical explanation for my behaviour, but I just couldn't. All I know is that it seemed less painful to push you away, to know that you were out there somewhere, living, loving and following your life's purpose, than to lose you some other way…" Greg's voice trailed away and a tear slid from the corner of his eye.

Violet remembered the moment she left Earth, and she couldn't speak. Had he seen it happening? Or was his fear based on the time he had lost her in their past lives? She snuggled into his side, and neither of them spoke again. Silently, Greg reached out and turned out the light. Wrapped in each other's arms, they fell asleep.

*   *   *

How could she have messed things up so quickly? It seemed that this being human lark really wasn't as easy as she thought it might be. At the sound of a few coins hitting the ground next to her, Aria looked up at the kind stranger from her spot in the doorway and smiled, but they were already walking away.

It seemed that the horrible lady was in fact her step-mother, who had been itching to find a good reason to get rid of her for quite some time. When she had been sacked from the job she never turned up to (because she didn't have a clue where she worked, or in fact anything about Anna's life) the step-mother had convinced her dad that the only way she was ever going to learn was if they threw her out.

They hadn't even allowed her to take much with her. They'd given her half an hour to pack a few belongings, which were mostly warm clothes, then they had banished her from their lives.

No wonder Anna's soul had decided not to return. Aria couldn't imagine choosing to live with such an awful human being. She gathered the few coins and put them in her cup. She didn't quite yet have enough to buy any food, and her stomach rumbled. She thought about the camera in her bag, and whether she should sell it, so that she could feed herself for a few days, but she couldn't part with it, as it was her only way to record everything she could remember from her previous life.

"Why don't you just get a job or something?" someone spat at her as they walked past. "Filthy scum littering the streets."

Aria felt her cheeks redden and she swallowed back tears. She knew she looked a little straggly, but she was doing her best not to litter. After all, Faeries never littered! She always made sure she cleaned up after herself.

Deciding that perhaps it would be a good idea to move on, she gathered up her bag and few belongings, and walked toward the park. As she walked, her mind raced with the possibilities of her next step. Despite feeling very sad and lonely, sleeping out in the cold, she knew that giving up and returning to the Other Side was not an option. Because Linen was here, somewhere, on Earth. And she would not give up until she found him. She had loved their relationship in their Faerie forms, but she was so curious what it would be like to be in a human relationship, that her curiosity was winning over her fear, sadness and feeling totally out of her depth.

When she reached the park, her spirits lifted, and she smiled. The low winter sun was filtering through the trees, and she wished she could dance, carefree and barefoot on the grass, and be a part of the Elemental Realm again, even if it were just for a few moments.

Aria stopped suddenly and frowned. Why couldn't she dance barefoot and carefree? What was stopping her? Okay, so it was the middle of winter, she had no home, no family, no money and her stomach was rumbling uncomfortably. But she was still alive wasn't she? She was still able to smile and laugh and sing and appreciate the world around her.

Without hesitating another moment, she ran over to the edge of the well-kept lawns and set her belongings down in a heap. She slipped off her shoes and her coat and added them to the pile. She shivered in the chilly breeze, but knew she would be warm enough soon.

She tiptoed across the icy grass, whispering apologies to the Faeries as she did so, even though she knew they were in a different dimensional plane to her, so she couldn't hurt them. She told them that she was going to dance among them, and then she closed her eyes and began to move to the music she heard in her mind.

She saw Linen sat at the piano, playing her song. She twirled and moved gracefully, using every part of her body and soul to express the love and happiness she felt in Linen's presence. She was so absorbed in her movement, in the feeling of the grass beneath her feet, and the soulful notes in her mind, that she was completely unaware of her audience until she came to a stop and heard the round of applause. She opened her eyes and saw that a crowd of people had gathered to watch her silent dance.

She blushed for the second time that afternoon, this time with pleasure. She smiled shyly at the crowd and did a little curtsy, earning her more applause. Several of the strangers then put coins into her cup, which she had left with her belongings. When she went over to retrieve her things, the crowd disbursed, but one member of the impromptu audience remained.

"Are you a trained dancer?" the man asked curiously.

Aria laughed. "No," she replied, then frowned. She had no recollection of Anna's life, perhaps she had been a dancer? "I mean, not really, I mean, well, I just like doing it," she finished, feeling foolish. She slipped on her shoes and coat, gathered up her things and picked up her cup, which had more than enough coins to buy her a meal. Her eyes lit up and her stomach rumbled in agreement.

"Trained or not, I think you dance beautifully," the stranger continued.

"Thank you," Aria said, blushing again.

The stranger started to turn away, but seemed to change his mind and turned back. "It doesn't involve dancing, but if you're looking for work, give me a call. I'm quite short-staffed at the moment and I think you would be perfect." He scribbled his number on a piece of paper and handed it to her. He smiled at her before starting to walk away.

"Wait," she called out. "What kind of job? Only I don't actually have anywhere to live right now, and I don't have a job because I don't have any skills in anything, and apparently I'm not very reliable…" her voice trailed off and she wished she hadn't been so honest. There was no way he would give her a job now she had openly admitted to being a complete flake.

But his reaction surprised her. He chuckled at her expression, but his face quickly turned serious. "Do you really have nowhere to live? I thought maybe you were just a student or something, making some extra cash."

She shook her head. "No, I'm not a student. I was living with my dad and step-mother, but when I got sacked from my job they threw me out. I've been sleeping anywhere I can for the last few nights. Usually on the grass, because it's softer than concrete and I feel more at home when I'm surrounded by trees." Aria forced herself to stop talking, for fear that she would sound a bit crazy and scare the man away.

"Come on then, come with me. I'll find you a place to stay and then we can discuss that job I mentioned."

Aria raised her eyebrows. "You're going to help me? But why? You don't even know me."

The stranger chuckled again. "What's your name?"

"Aria. What's yours?"

"Tim." He held out his hand, and she shook it. "Nice to meet you, Aria. Now we know each other." He smiled. "To be honest, I just get the feeling that we have met before, and that it's important I help you. Besides, if you're interested in the job, you would be helping me out a lot too."

Aria thought about it for a moment. She knew that perhaps it was not a normal thing for humans to do, to just trust a total stranger, but then she wasn't really human, and she most certainly wasn't normal, so it made sense to go with it. Besides, she could tell that he was a good soul. And he did seem quite familiar to her, even though she wasn't sure why.

"Okay, Tim. I'll come with you."

Tim smiled and together they set off down the path. They hadn't walked more than a few steps before Aria started chattering away.

*   *   *

"Who are you and what have you done with my son?"

Charlie looked up at his mum, who was watching him suspiciously as he took a black bag full of rubbish out to the wheelie bin. He walked back toward her, a smile on his face. "Just doing a bit of cleaning in my room."

She raised her eyebrows nearly to her hairline. "Since when do you do any kind of cleaning at all?"

"Since I realised I was living like a complete pig, and I needed to change things." He kissed her on the head as he passed her in the kitchen doorway, and she watched him go back inside, her mouth wide open in shock.

He chuckled all the way up the stairs, but when he re-entered his bedroom, he sighed. There was still quite a long way to go yet. He switched on his laptop and started listing all of his computer games for sale. And the games console. It took him several hours of photographing and writing the descriptions and listings, but when he had finished, he was confident that they should sell quite quickly. Once done, he sat for a while, drumming his fingers on the desktop.

What was he going to fill his time with now? He figured he could get a job, maybe earn some money so he could get his own place at some point. He loved his mum, but it wasn't exactly the most attractive position to be in to meet a girl.

He recalled the crazy vision he'd had, which had sparked these massive changes in his personality. After his initial overwhelming feelings of grief and sadness, it was as though it had opened a doorway in his mind, because since then, he kept getting visions of another place, another time. White corridors, amazingly surreal gardens with gold statues, and as much as he couldn't even believe it himself, Faeries and Angels.

At first he wondered if he was going mad, or having some bizarre hallucinations, brought on by too many E-numbers in the massive amount of junk food he liked to consume. But the visions seemed so real, and so detailed, he didn't think they could be purely created by his own imagination.

Also, he had seen Violet in them. She looked much older, but it was her, he was sure of it. And the beautiful woman he had glimpsed in the original vision had been there too. Again, only very briefly, but he was sure it was her.

What it all meant, he still wasn't entirely sure. But he figured that if it inspired him to change, inspired him to live a better life, then perhaps it didn't matter what it meant.

He got up from his desk and continued to clean up, throwing items he no longer wanted into a box. He planned to take it to a charity shop and from now on, he wanted to minimalise his room, so that he had the space to think.

Another hour later, he had to turn the light on in order to continue. His room was looking the best it ever had. He checked his listings and found that people were already bidding on the items. Rather than allowing his mum to eat alone, as she did every evening while he ate in his room and continued to play his games, he went downstairs to join her.

Her shock at his sudden change in behaviour soon made way for joy as they had an actual conversation with each other while eating. Charlie couldn't remember the last time he had heard his mother laugh, and that realisation created a lump in his throat that made it difficult for him to finish his meal. When they finished, he insisted on doing the washing up, while she went to watch her favourite programmes on TV. As she passed him in the kitchen on her way to the lounge, she hugged him from behind.

"Thank you, Charlie, for such a lovely evening," she said, her voice wavering a little. He turned around and pulled her into a proper hug, his large frame engulfing her tiny one.

"I'm sorry I haven't been a good person, Mum. But that's all going to change now, I promise."

He felt his mother nod, then she pulled away and went to the lounge. He knew that she was crying, and didn't want him to see. He wiped his own tears on the back of his hand, then finished the dishes. He joined her in the lounge, and spent the whole evening watching mindless soap operas with her. Every few minutes, he could sense her sneaking a look at him, and he wondered if she genuinely thought he had been taken over by an alien of some kind.

When he realised that she had fallen asleep on the sofa, he switched off the TV, covered her with a blanket and then kissed her on the forehead before heading upstairs.

Back in his room, he lay on top of the covers on his bed and reached down the side for the box he had hidden there. He pulled it out and opened it. He took out the photograph that sat on the very top.

He gazed at Violet's face, and wondered if she ever had been truly happy with him, or whether her bright smile had just been covering up her pain. He searched her eyes for answers, but found only more questions. Where was she now?

Who was she with? He had not spoken to her since she had thrown him out. And a few months later, he had walked past her house and saw that different people lived there. He had no idea how he would get back in touch with her.

Not that he wanted to. She had made it quite plain that she was not interested in ever seeing him again, and as much of an asshole as he had been to her during their relationship, he wanted to respect her wishes, and do at least one decent thing by her.

He sighed, tucked the photograph into the box, and slid it back into its hiding place. He switched off his bedside lamp and lay awake for a long time, staring into the darkness.

*   *   *

"Let me get this straight, you have lost all forms of ID and need to get new ones?"

"Yes, that is correct. My bag was stolen with all of my documents in, and I am between homes right now too, so I have no address either."

"Between homes?" The incredulous look on the passport office worker's face was so comical that Starlight had to fight back a giggle.

"That's right," she confirmed with a straight face.

The man, whose name badge said 'Tony' shook his head. "How do you expect me to issue you with a passport when you have nothing to prove who you are? Do you have any old bills in your name? Any paperwork at all?"

"I'm afraid my house burned down. I lost everything."

"Right. Yeah, of course it did. Look, I'm going to have to get my supervisor, because I'm not really sure what to do here, just because you sound English, doesn't mean that you are. I would get sacked for issuing a passport with no ID at all. You could be some kind of foreign spy or something."

"That's okay, Tony. I completely understand. I will wait

here to speak to your supervisor."

With a perplexed look on his face, Tony picked up his phone and dialled a number. After a few muttered words, he set the phone down and looked up at Starlight. "Just have a seat, she'll be right out with you."

"Thank you, Tony, for all your help."

Starlight sat down in the waiting area, and when she heard a door opening, she looked up and smiled when she saw who came through it. Starlight stood up to greet her, and the shock on the supervisor's face was priceless. She recovered pretty quickly, and ushered her into the back office, with Tony looking on with interest while dealing with the next person in line.

Once safely in the office, she suddenly threw her arms around the Angel. "Starlight!" she exclaimed. "Is it really you?"

Starlight hugged her back and chuckled. "My dear Indigo, it is indeed me. You have done well for yourself, I am so proud of you."

The Indigo Child released her and shook her head. "I'm not so sure about that. I stupidly thought that I would be able to change things here, but I was so wrong."

"You are in the perfect place. Without you, getting myself a new identity would not be possible."

"So you are here to stay? You're not just dropping in?" the Indigo, whose name badge said 'Hannah', asked.

"I am here to stay," Starlight confirmed. "With the world getting to re-do the next twenty years, I knew I needed to be here, to make sure the outcome was different this time."

"I knew it! I knew that time had been messed with! All the Indigos and Earth Angels I know have experienced it. What is going on?"

"In the original time-line, Velvet left Earth and re-entered the Other Side. She then came home to me, to the stars. After twenty years, the world ended, and Velvet decided that she shouldn't have left. So she got Gold to let her go back in time for a second chance."

"Wow. That is even crazier than I imagined. So the world isn't going to end in twenty years' time now?"

"Not if I have anything to do with it. But right now, I need your assistance in creating new documents in order for me to work and live here, and help in any way I can."

"Of course! I can get all of that sorted for you. Do you have a name?" Hannah frowned. "You're not a walk-in, surely? You look too much like yourself."

"I am not a walk-in, I entered Earth in my own body. I just made it a little denser than normal. I haven't thought much about names. I guess 'Starlight' is a little too way out?" She smiled, only half-joking.

"I've heard weirder names in this job, trust me. How about Sarah? It's a popular name, you'll blend in."

Starlight nodded her assent and Hannah began to tap information into her computer. "What about money? And a place to live? If you haven't got anything yet, I would be honoured to help you get set up."

"My dear, beautiful Indigo, that would be amazing. I would love your assistance."

"Brilliant. I will get all your paperwork sorted, and I have some friends who can sort out NI numbers, birth certificates, etcetera." She winked at Starlight. "I have friends in high places."

"Me too," Starlight replied, thinking of Gold.

*   *   *

"Greg! Thank goodness you finally called, I was going nuts wondering what was going on!" Leona could almost hear Greg's wince over the phone.

"Lee, I'm so sorry, I should have got in touch sooner, it's just been so crazy. I didn't stop to think that you must be going out of your mind."

Leona tutted, but was only half-serious. "Typical male. So what happened? Did you find Violet?"

"Yes, she was in the middle of nowhere, at a retreat with her friends. I'm still there actually, I'm using their phone, so I can't be too long."

"Okay, so just tell me quickly – what's happening with you two now?"

"Always straight to the point," Greg chuckled. "We're back together. She has forgiven me for my crazy actions, and we are going to give us a second chance."

Leona pumped her fist into the air and did a little dance, getting herself tangled up in the phone wire as she did so. "That's brilliant!" she said, trying to control her enthusiasm a little. "I'm so very happy for you guys, you really are an amazing couple."

"Thank you. Violet and Amy say hi, and we haven't figured out our next step yet, but I will do my best to keep you better informed, I promise. Have you got a pen and paper? I'll give you Violet's mobile number."

Leona grabbed the nearest writing implement, and scribbled the number down. "Thank you, that'll stop me going crazy. Now go, before you rack up a massive phone bill."

"Yes, okay, it's good to hear your voice, Leona, I'll speak to you again soon."

"You too, bye, Greg."

"Bye."

Leona hung up the phone and stared at it for a few seconds. Although she was ecstatic that they had got back together, she also couldn't quite believe it at the same time. What had convinced Greg that he and Violet should be together? She wondered if he had experienced a similar crazy vision as she had, and perhaps that had brought about his sudden Awakening. She would have to ask him about it the next time she saw him, whenever that would be.

She looked at the calendar next to the phone and realised that the owners of the house would be back in two days, at which point, she would need to move on. Without Greg and his campervan, it seemed she would have to continue her travelling alone and on foot, which was how she originally started off before they met on the ferry.

But that was okay, part of her wanted to head for the major cities, to see if she could match a place to her vision. She felt a sudden, deep longing to find the person she had seen, because she knew that when she did, she would feel like she had finally come home.

Chapter Three

"I'm so incredibly pleased for you both, Violet," Esmeralda said, as they hugged. "Greg seems like a wonderful man, and it appears that he has finally Awoken. I really do wish the both of you all the love and luck in the world."

Violet squeezed Esmeralda in return. "Thank you. It's been so amazing to be here with you, and my Spiritual Sisters had an amazing time too. I know they all wish they could have stayed longer."

Esmeralda pulled away and smiled. "They know they are all welcome back at any time. As are you both." She turned to Greg and hugged him. "You look after my friend now, won't you?" she whispered to him.

"I will, I promise."

"Right then, Mike is around somewhere, goodness knows where, hopefully you will see him on your way out."

Violet smiled. "I hope so. I want to thank him too." She took the hand that Greg offered her, and they set off down the path to the campervan. Violet looked over her shoulder and waved goodbye again to Esmeralda, who was watching them leave. She felt sad to be leaving this sacred place, but they couldn't stay forever, there were more guests booked in and more Earth Angels in need of help to find their Twin Flames.

It seemed quite funny really, to have come alone to a Twin

Flame retreat, only to leave hand in hand with her real life Flame. She giggled to herself, wondering what the odds were.

"What's so funny?" Greg asked, as they let go of each other in order to climb into the van.

Violet sat in the passenger seat and inhaled the familiar scent of the camper, which brought back a thousand happy memories. "Oh, nothing, I was just thinking about us coming back together at a Twin Flame retreat. If only every Earth Angel who visited here could do the same, it would be quite amazing."

Greg chuckled. "Yes, it would be quite the selling point to guarantee meeting your Flame here. They'd be booked up every day of the week."

Violet smiled as he reached across and squeezed her knee, it was such a loving and familiar gesture, she hadn't realised how many small things he did that she had missed during the previous few months. "So where to now?"

Greg shrugged. "We'll need to go back to Amy's parents', I assume, to collect your things?" Violet nodded. "And, well, I think I should pay my ex and kids a visit."

Violet's eyes widened. "Really?" In all the months they had been travelling, he wouldn't even talk about them, let alone entertain the idea of getting in touch or visiting them. "Why now?"

"Why not? I'd hate to think of the girls growing up believing that I was dead or something. Not that I believe that I am actually their dad, but still, I'm sure they would feel better if they knew I was okay. And I would like to apologise for the way I left."

Violet was silent for a while. She didn't know what to say. "If you want me to come with you, I will."

Greg smiled and started up the engine. "Thank you, but I think maybe I need to do this alone. So maybe the next step should be to go back to Amy's, I'll make my visit, then I'll come back to you and we'll make our plans from there."

Violet nodded and put her seatbelt on. Though her stomach was clenching at the thought of having to let go of Greg even just for a day, she knew that he needed to have that closure. "Yes, I think that sounds like a plan."

As Greg reversed and then pulled into the bumpy lane to leave the retreat, Violet saw movement through the window among the trees.

"Wait," she said to Greg. He stopped and she wound the window down to speak to Mike.

"Hey, you two," he said. "Thought you were going to slip away without saying goodbye?"

Violet laughed. "Sorry, Mike, we just thought we'd better get moving. Besides, I'm sure we will be back to see you soon enough." Suddenly, Violet had an image flash through her mind, of the three of them stood around a bed, and Mike was crying. She blinked and the image disappeared as fast as it came. Without really understanding why, she undid her seatbelt, got out of the van and hugged Mike hard. He seemed a little surprised, but hugged her back anyway. "If you ever need us, at any time, just call, okay? You have my mobile number don't you?"

"Of course," he said.

Violet pulled away and smiled up at him. "Good." She felt on the edge of tears as she climbed back into the van, and closed the door.

"Thanks for everything, Mike. See you soon," Greg said.

"Yeah, see you soon," Mike echoed, still looking at Violet with confusion. She smiled back at him, and they pulled away, making their way slowly down the lane.

"What was that about?" Greg asked, sensing that Violet was feeling quite emotional.

"I don't know," she replied. "I just got the feeling that we would be seeing them again, and a lot sooner than we think."

"Oh," Greg said, not really understanding. "That's good isn't it?"

Violet couldn't answer. Instead, she leaned over to the old stereo and fiddled with the radio until she found a decent station.

Realising that she wasn't in the mood to talk, Greg just rested his hand back on her knee, and grateful for his silence, she rested her hand on top of his.

*   *   *

Aria sat at the table, clutching her bag, while Tim made a cup of tea and set it in front of her. "I still don't know why you are helping me," she said.

Tim smiled and sat across from her. "I guess I just like helping people. And you looked like you needed a break. How long have you been homeless?"

Aria shrugged. "Just a few days. It wasn't too bad, though it got pretty cold at night. I think I wore every bit of clothing I had with me and was still shivery. I met some other people who have been homeless for a long time. I don't really know how they do it."

"Me either. I've been very lucky not to be in that position, I can't imagine how it must feel."

"It's not very nice," Aria said quietly. She picked up the mug and sipped a little of the tea; it was too hot to gulp down as she wanted to. "I'm not really sure I like this being human lark," she muttered.

"Being human?" Tim asked, his curiosity peaked. "What do you mean?"

Aria frowned. "If I explain, you might think I'm crazy, then you might not give me the job, whatever the job is, then I might end up back out in the cold again."

"I don't go back on my word," Tim reassured her. "I'm sure whatever you have to say isn't going to change my opinion of you."

Aria stared at him for a while, then relented. "It's probably easier if you watch the video I recorded. I explain it all in that." She dug around in her bag and pulled the camera out, handing it to Tim.

He took the memory card out, then he went over to his desk and put the card in his laptop. Aria stayed seated at the table, drinking her tea while he watched the video she'd made on her first day as a human. He didn't utter a word throughout the whole twenty-five minutes, and when the screen went black, Aria waited impatiently to hear what he thought, but he remained motionless, staring at the screen. Slowly he turned to face her, and she was surprised to see that he was crying.

"Are you okay?" she asked. She hadn't shown anyone the video before, and if this was how people were going to react, she wasn't sure she ever would again.

"Aria," he whispered. The way he said her name made her frown.

"What?" she asked.

"I was there. At the Academy. I remember it. And I remember you now too."

Her eyebrows shot up. "You did? You do? Really?"

"You were a Faerie, you grew grass in the Elemental Realm."

"I know, I just said all of that in the video." Aria was beginning to wonder if he was just playing around with her, or worse, humouring her.

"You were afraid of becoming human, so you decided to stay at the Academy. Your best friend was an Angel, called Amethyst, and you had another roommate. A Starperson, called-"

"Tim!" Aria's hand flew to her mouth. "How do you have the same name?" She knew it was a stupid question as soon as she asked it, but she was still curious.

"Tim isn't my given human name, I changed it to Tim because I preferred it." He shook his head. "I've been having these dreams, these glimpses of the past all my life, and part of me just felt that perhaps I was a little crazy. That maybe I was just meant to be a sci-fi writer or something. I remember being on another planet, and I remember being at the Academy, but this is the first time in my entire life that I have admitted any of this to anyone."

"Wow. I can't imagine not ever being able to tell anyone who I am," Aria said, her face sad. "I never want to have to pretend I'm someone or something I'm not. I guess that's why I ended up without a home."

"So how are you here? You're a walk-in now?" Tim gestured to the laptop screen. "What does that mean anyway?"

"It means that I swapped places with another soul, I took over their body. They wanted to stay on the Other Side, and I wanted to try out the human thing for a while."

"Wow, I didn't even know that was possible."

"Well, as Gold is fond of saying, anything is possible. All I need to do is find Linen, and then everything will be okay again."

"Linen? The assistant to the head of the Academy?"

"Yes." Aria smiled. "He's my Twin Flame. We walked in together. But I don't really know anything about the soul he swapped with. Or if I did know, I don't remember. All I know is we chose them because they were geographically close and they were in situations where it would be possible to be together again."

"That's amazing. I don't know how useful I can be, but I will do what I can to help you find Linen. And of course, you can stay here for as long as you need to."

Aria smiled. "You are the most helpful alien ever! Thank you, you're making the human thing a little more bearable."

Tim chuckled. "Good. Now, I don't know about you, but I think I need to get some sleep. You can have the spare room, it's all made up ready. If you need anything, let me know, or just have a rummage in the cupboards. Make yourself at home, okay?"

Aria's eyes filled with tears at the mention of home, and she nodded, trying not to cry. Tim switched his laptop off and left the room, passing her and squeezing her shoulder as he did.

"Good night, Faerie," he said.

She smiled. "Good night, Alien."

*　　*　　*

Despite his complete transformation that had taken place practically overnight, Charlie still couldn't quite believe that he was in the Mind, Body, Spirit section of his local bookstore, looking at books about Angels and Faeries, and trying to decide which ones to buy. A couple of times, he had considered whether he should go to the doctors and ask if he could be referred for therapy, because he felt a little like he was losing his mind, but knowing that his doctor would probably just medicate him instead, he had opted to visit the bookshop.

"Do you like that author?"

His head snapped around, and he felt like he had been caught, that his secret was out. When he saw the face that belonged to the voice, he dropped the books.

The beautiful woman from his vision laughed. "Sorry, didn't mean to startle you." When he continued to stare at her in shock, unable to form any words, she frowned and stepped closer to him. "Have we met before?"

Wide-eyed still, Charlie managed to finally blink and clear his throat. "Um, no, I don't think we have." He held out his hand. "My name's Charlie."

She took his hand and shook it. "Nice to meet you, Charlie. I'm Ceri."

When their hands made contact, they both gasped a little. They held on much longer than the usual length of time for a handshake, and stared into each other's eyes. It wasn't until someone asked if they could get past them to the bookshelf that they broke out of their trance.

Ceri laughed nervously and pulled her hand away. She bent down to pick up the books he had dropped, and handed them to him. Charlie took them, and tried to think of something to say.

"Would you like to have a drink with me?" The words were out of his mouth before he could think them through, and he hoped she didn't think he was too forward.

She smiled. "I would love to. Are you going to buy those first?"

Charlie looked down at the books. "Yes, I am."

They went over to the counter, and Charlie paid for the books, using some of the money he'd made from selling his video games. They left the bookshop and headed for the café across the road. Once settled, they ordered drinks, then Ceri broke the silence.

"Why do you seem so familiar to me?"

It seemed he wasn't the only forthright one. He shook his head, unwilling to admit that he had seen her in a vision. "Perhaps we met in a past life," he joked.

"That's not such a crazy concept," Ceri said, accepting her drink from the waitress with a smile of gratitude. "Have you ever had a past life regression?"

Charlie shook his head. "No, to be honest, all of this spiritual stuff is a completely new thing for me. Up until recently, I really had no interest in it at all."

"That's cool. I've only been into it for the last few years, I just find it all so fascinating. I have read everything I can get my hands on. I love that there are still new things to learn, to discover, and I love it when I read something that just blows my mind."

Charlie sipped his coffee and pondered her words. "I guess I have had a few experiences recently that have blown my mind a little."

"That's a good thing. Are those experiences what set you on this path?"

"Yes, they were a massive wake-up call."

Ceri placed her hand over his. "Well, I for one, am glad that you have Awakened, Charlie."

He smiled, enjoying her touch. "Me too."

*   *   *

"Dear Gold, we understand your feelings of grief, but it really won't be long until you are reunited."

Even the soft, encouraging words of the Rainbows couldn't heal Gold's broken heart. He was sat in room 334 at the Academy, surrounded by the dancing light beams, holding one of the Rainbows in his weathered hand.

"But I live for those moments," he whispered. "Those beautiful moments when she appears before me, and bestows her wisdom. Those beautiful moments when she takes a soul home to the stars. Those wondrous moments when I call her name and she is immediately by my side, the stars in her wings lighting up my soul. How can I continue my existence without those moments?"

The Rainbows were silent for a few seconds, while they danced around the forlorn man sat amongst them. The Rainbow he held, shimmered and shivered, and he thought that perhaps they had no more wisdom to offer him. Just as he was about to open his hand and let it go, they spoke once more.

"You can choose to. You can choose to continue existing without those moments. What would you do otherwise?"

It was Gold's turn to be quiet. They had a point. What would be the use of returning home to the stars, while she was not there? And what would be the point of going to Earth, when all his best souls were already there doing all they could? He looked around the room, and a thought struck him then. The Academy now seemed so empty without Linen and Aria.

All of the souls who had wished to return to re-live the twenty years had already gone. And those who wished to move on had done so. There was no one left but himself and the Rainbows. But perhaps there was a reason for this?

"Is there a purpose for me here?" he asked the tiny light in his palm. "Is there a reason why I have been left behind?"

"Yes, Gold, there is."

"What is it?"

"Visit Velvet and Laguz, and all will become apparent."

Gold frowned. "What do you mean?"

But the Rainbow danced out of his hand and away from him without answering. He sat and watched them for a while, then stood slowly, feeling an uncomfortable ache from sitting on the floor. He stretched out his limbs, then waved goodbye to the tiny lights.

Out in the hallway, he mulled over their words. Did they mean for him to visit the statues of Velvet and Laguz? Without thinking it through further, he closed his eyes and silently reappeared in the Atlantis Garden. He sat on the golden, jewel-encrusted bench, and stared at the marble statues of the two Flames. Their hands were entwined, and Velvet's eyes were on her beloved. Even in marble, he could see and feel the absolute, pure unconditional love that Velvet had for Laguz. He had no doubt that now they were together, they would see that the Flames were reunited on Earth. Because truly, it was only that kind of love that could possibly save humankind.

He wondered how it had all gone so terribly pear-shaped. How could it be that killing another was seen as acceptable in any situation? How could wars be seen as a solution to any problem? How could the stealing of innocence be seen as a right bestowed to anyone? It weighed down his heart to think of some of the suffering and sorrow some souls had experienced. Of course, by the time they reached him, waiting for them on the Other Side, all of that had been stripped away, leaving nothing but their purest light.

He had never told anyone in existence this, but when all the pain was stripped from them, he would take on a small part of it, into his own soul. And that was why he had aged. He knew that to truly understand them, he had to experience some of what they had experienced. It was only fair – after all, they were on that planet because of himself and the other Elders. It didn't seem right to him, not to take on some of their sorrow. It would feel too much like he was a dictator, sending his best and most beautiful into a war he knew they would never win.

He brought his attention back to the present moment, to the statues of his bravest soldiers, and he sighed. He had not yet become aware of his new purpose, his new mission. Perhaps this was not what the Rainbows meant? He got up from the bench and approached the figures, studying them for a while. He noticed that a rune pendant hung from Velvet's neck, and he traced the symbol, the rune of laguz, in the simple wooden shape. He knew that the rune pendant had been instrumental in their reunion, that it was what led Velvet to recognise her Flame.

Without fully understanding why, Gold reached up and removed the necklace from Velvet, replacing it around his own neck. As soon as it settled into place, he felt a sense of comfort, of knowing that he and Starlight would indeed get their chance to be together again. He still had no idea of his new purpose, but that didn't seem to matter, for now, he would just do his work, welcoming souls to the Other Side, and he would stay open to any ideas that appeared.

"Gold."

He jumped at the sound of his name and the touch on his arm, and turned to see an Indigo Child staring up at him. He frowned. Most of the Indigo and Crystal Children, who had yet to be born in the new twenty-year span, had decided to return home to their planets to visit their kin while waiting to re-enter Earth, rather than remain at the Academy. He hadn't realised there were any still there.

"My sweet Indigo, what is it?" he asked, immediately lowering himself to have eye contact with the beautiful child.

The Indigo reached out to touch the pendant he now wore, then looked up to see Velvet's bare neck. "I had the feeling that I should remain here, rather than go with my siblings back to the Indigo World. When I asked the Rainbows, to tell me my purpose, all I got was 'Gold'. I thought they were referencing the Golden Age, but I think they meant you."

Gold frowned. "Me? I'm your purpose? How does that make sense?"

"I do not yet know. But I feel that it is important that I spend time with you. If you are amenable to that, of course."

Gold shrugged, but his right eye twitched slightly, giving away his nervousness over the idea. "I was simply planning to return to the mists, and continue my work there. You are welcome to come with me, but I'm not sure what you will get from it."

"It is not part of my purpose to get anything. I am here to give."

Gold smiled and held out his hand to the Child. "Come with me, my Child. We will attempt to work this out together."

The Indigo Child placed her tiny hand in Gold's, and within the blink of an eye, they left the Atlantis Garden, and returned to the mists at the edge of the Fifth Dimension.

*   *   *

"Merci beaucoup," Leona said to the waitress who set the steaming hot chocolate in front of her. It felt good to sit down after several hours of travelling. She had decided to head to Paris after leaving La Rochelle, and after resting a little, she planned to find her HelpX host's place, leave her rucksack there and then explore the city.

She tried to kid herself, and pretend that she was just intrigued by the history and the architecture of the city, but in truth, she really just wanted to match a real place to her vision of her Flame. Since she'd had the twenty-year long vision, she had been haunted every night in her dreams by those piercing eyes, and she felt like she was going a little bit mad.

She sipped the hot chocolate, and closed her eyes in bliss, momentarily distracted. She thought of Greg. Despite his promise to stay in touch, she hadn't heard from him in several days. She had sent a text to Violet's phone to let them know that she was moving on from the cottage, and that she was heading to Paris. She didn't know if he and Violet would come back to Europe, and continue travelling, or if they would stay in the UK. And she'd had no visions of them to let her know what they would be doing.

By the time she had finished her drink, far from feeling rested, her mind felt frayed and muddled. With a sigh, she left a tip for the waitress, then headed out of the small café, and after consulting her city map, she headed in the direction of her host's home.

It took her a lot longer to reach it than she had expected, but that could have been because she was scanning every building, every sign, and the skyline as she walked, trying to recognise something. Anything. When she reached the apartment, and her host let her in, she was so tired, she couldn't even contemplate going back out to begin her search.

Her host provided her with a simple meal of French bread and cheese, and after eating, she excused herself and retired to the spare bed. Within moments of laying down, she was asleep.

Chapter Four

"Can I help you?"

Greg frowned. "I'm sorry, I think I have the wrong house, I was looking for Carly."

The man who had opened the door nodded slightly. "You have the right house, Carly's here, do you want me to call her?"

"Oh, um, yes, if you could." His heart started hammering, and his hands clenched and unclenched. He wished then that he had allowed Violet to come with him. He could have done with her support in that moment.

The man turned away from him and called out into the house. A few seconds later, Carly appeared, and when she saw Greg, she gasped and her hands flew to her mouth. She walked the last few steps toward him slowly, as if she didn't believe her eyes.

"Greg?" she whispered. When she was close enough, she reached out to touch his arm. When she was certain he was real, she flung herself into his arms, and shocked, he stood there, motionless, silent, not knowing what to do or say.

She sobbed onto his shoulder and he looked helplessly at the man stood in the doorway. Finally, he made himself wrap his arms around her, and embraced her until her sobs subsided. She pulled back a little then, and stared into his eyes. She searched them for a few seconds, then when she didn't find what she was looking for, she pulled back further and slapped him so hard he stumbled backward.

"You bastard," she spat, with so much venom that he took another step back. The man in the doorway reached out to her, and pulled her into his arms. She went willingly, allowing him to restrain her. "Get out of here before the girls come home. I don't want you to see them. And I don't want to ever see you again, do you hear me? You are not my husband anymore. I filed the papers when you never came back."

Greg nodded, feeling relieved at her words, yet feeling slightly confused by her reactions at the same time. He retreated backward down the path to his campervan. Once he was safely inside, he rubbed his sore cheek then started the engine. It rumbled to life and he pulled away from the kerb.

On the journey back to Amy's parents' house, he decided that he had more than deserved the slap, and that his visit had been a good thing. To know they were no longer married was a relief, and to know that she realised he was not the man she had loved and married, made him feel better.

He pulled up outside the house, his heart leaping in anticipation of seeing Violet again. He had only seen her that morning, but his heart had ached every moment they were apart.

He jumped out of the van and locked it, then made his way up the steps. Despite the low temperatures, perhaps she'd like to stay with him in the van that night, rather than in the house, where they might be disturbed.

The front door opened before he reached it, and light spilled out into the darkness. Greg smiled at Violet, and without needing to speak she opened her arms and they embraced. He breathed in the sweet scent of her hair, and knew that everything would be alright.

*   *   *

"So what do you think?"

Aria looked at Tim, having no idea what he had just asked. All she could think was that she was in heaven. A large blue butterfly landed on her hand, and she was mesmerised by it, forgetting that Tim even existed. After a few moments, he cleared his throat and the butterfly flew away.

"Do you want the job?"

Aria blinked, trying to pay attention. "You want me to play with butterflies all day?" she asked, not quite comprehending his offer.

Tim laughed. "Not quite. I would like you to be a tour guide for the Butterfly Zoo, among other things. We often do events for children, which I would like you to help with, and there will be the more boring work too, like working in the shop and selling tickets and cleaning. But I think you would enjoy it."

Aria frowned. "How did you know I would be good at this just by watching me dance in the park?"

"Because you looked like a butterfly. I knew you would fit right in. Of course, you will need to learn about all the different types of butterfly for the tour, but I'm sure that won't be a problem for a Faerie."

Aria laughed. "I already know them all! All of the Faeries had to learn the proper names of their friends, it's only polite after all. But just one thing, I had dragonfly wings, not butterfly wings."

Tim held a hand up. "I do apologise, of course you did. So if you already know about the different types, it should be easy for you. Would you like to start immediately? We're quite short-staffed at the moment."

"Definitely! What do you want me to do?"

"Come with me, you can shadow one of the other staff for the day, and they will show you all you need to know." Tim walked down the flower-lined path of the butterfly enclosure, and Aria followed reluctantly, not wanting to leave just yet.

"I'll be back," she whispered.

*　　*　　*

"Mum, there's someone I would like you to meet."

Without any prompting, Ceri immediately approached Charlie's mum and embraced her. Charlie could see the slightly surprised look on his mum's face over Ceri's shoulder.

"Nice to meet you," she said, when Ceri released her. "Who are you?"

Ceri chuckled. "My name is Ceri. I met Charlie just a couple of days ago, in the bookshop."

Charlie couldn't tell if the look of confusion on his mum's face was due to the fact that her son had been inside a bookshop, or because he had just brought a girl home for the first time ever.

"Ceri and I were going out for the day, but she wanted to meet you first, I hope that's okay."

Still in a state of shock and confusion, his mum tried to regain her composure. "Of course. It was nice to meet you. I hope you both have a lovely day."

"Thanks, Mum." Charlie gave his mum a quick hug, then led Ceri out of the back door. As they walked down the path to the street, she reached out and took his hand. He looked down at their entwined fingers, then smiled at her. "I think she was a little surprised."

Ceri laughed. "I think she was. But then, from what you have told me, you have been through quite a massive transformation recently."

"I have, I don't think she's quite adapted to it yet, but I'm sure she will. I think maybe she's waiting for the old me to come back at any moment."

Ceri tightened her grip on his hand. "You shouldn't bottle anything up, you know. If you feel the need to be angry, then you should find a way to do that. If you keep it all inside, it will eat you away."

Flashes of his vision came back to him then, of being eaten away by cancer, in his anger and sadness at losing Violet. His stomach clenched. He had no idea if she was okay, or where she was. He hoped that his vision had not come true, and that she was still on this Earthly plane.

"What is it?" Ceri stopped them in their tracks and turned to face him.

He closed his eyes and shook his head. "How is it that we have only just met, yet you can read me so easily?"

She shrugged. "I don't know. I just sensed then, that your energy changed, there was a darkness that descended." She shook her head. "I don't know how else to describe it."

"I was thinking of someone, from my past, and how I don't know if they're okay, and how much I miss them," he said, careful not to let on that he was talking about a girlfriend.

Ceri looked deep into his eyes, making him feel like she was reading his soul like a book. "She meant a lot to you," she whispered.

His eyes widened. How could she know that?

"But it wasn't right, something was wrong, and so she left," Ceri continued. She smiled and reached up to stroke his cheek. "It wasn't your fault. It was never meant to be."

For the first time since he had collapsed after his vision, Charlie felt tears well up in his eyes, and a single tear rolled down his cheek. "How do you know that?"

Ceri smiled. "Because I know you. And I know that you didn't mean to cause her any harm."

Unable to contain himself any longer, Charlie allowed the tears to fall freely, and Ceri stepped forward to embrace him, her arms making him feel safe, even though her slender frame was eclipsed by his. Ignoring the fact that they were stood on the pavement, in public, in the middle of the day, Charlie allowed himself to release all of the worries and fears he had been holding inside since his vision.

When his tears began to slow, he squeezed Ceri tightly, and thanked the Angels for bringing her shining light into his life.

"I am thankful for you, too," Ceri whispered into his ear.

*   *   *

Though she had visited Earth on many occasions in her Angelic form, being a wingless human was something quite different. Starlight sipped her hot drink, tasting the slight bitterness of the beverage called coffee, and stared out of the window. The busy city streets below her hummed with life, as the humans and most likely, Earth Angels, went about their day.

She was staying with Hannah, the very accommodating Indigo Child who had created a whole new identity for her. She looked down at the table, where her new passport lay open. The photograph looked nothing like her. It had completely failed to capture her otherworldly radiance. But at least it would allow her to live and work there, and to travel around.

She sipped more of her coffee, and wondered what to do with the day. Though she knew her main purpose was to assist Velvet with the Awakening, she had not figured out the smaller details of her mission, preferring to go with the flow and see what opportunities arose. It seemed almost comical, that the Angel of Destiny was entrusting her own destiny to the whim of the humans around her. But it felt like the right thing to do.

She decided to get dressed and explore the city. Perhaps she would receive some inspiration while meeting people and finding her way around her new home.

After finishing the drink, and wincing at the harshness of it, she dressed in the clothing that Hannah had found for her, took the spare key and some cash, then set off.

Once out on the pavement, she breathed in deeply and followed her intuition down the road toward the main busy street. It was a bizarre experience, being seen, being human, being a normal person on a normal street. Once she got used to weaving in and out of the crowds, and being jostled and nudged by strangers passing by, she began to enjoy herself. Though they did not realise it, these strangers were all connecting with one another, all creating an invisible web of energy.

A couple of times, she recognised Earth Angels, and wondered if they knew of their true origins. Considering the glazed look in their eyes, she guessed that they didn't. Perhaps that was to be the first part of her mission, to Awaken those who were still asleep to their true selves.

Without a thought as to why, she suddenly veered off the main street down a small alleyway, and found herself outside a tiny store-front with a sign in the window that said:

"Meditation Class - Meet your Guardian Angel. This Thursday at 12pm."

Starlight had no idea what day it was, or even what time it was, but she entered the store, knowing that this was exactly where she needed to be.

"Hi! Are you here for the meditation? They're just out in the back room, they haven't quite started yet."

Starlight nodded to the kind lady behind the counter, and followed her gesture toward the back of the shop, going through a beaded curtain and into a small back room that had no windows and was lit by candlelight.

Four women and two men were sat on cushions on the floor in a circle, and all but one of the ladies had their eyes closed. She saw Starlight by the door and invited her to take up the final remaining cushion on the floor. As Starlight sat down, she could sense the lady looking at her more intensely, a slight frown on her serene features. Starlight closed her eyes, and the lady spoke, beginning the meditation.

"I am going to count down from ten, and as I do, I want you to imagine that you are becoming lighter and lighter, until you feel like you are floating. Nine, you can feel a tingling throughout your body, eight, the burdens of the day are lifting from your shoulders, seven…"

As Starlight listened to her voice, she felt her body become lighter, and enjoyed the sensation. She'd only had a dense human body for a short time, but the weight of it did bother her.

"Now I want you to see yourself surrounded by a white mist. As you float forward, you will see a gate before you. There is an Angel at the gate, she has been waiting for you. She opens the gate and you float past her, down a winding pathway until you reach a pebbled beach beside a lake. The lake surface is so still, it is like glass…"

Starlight could see everything she described perfectly, because she had been there many times before. She wondered if the lady even realised that she had just described the entry into the Angelic Realm.

"Sat by the lake, is an Angel, they have been watching over you while you are on Earth, and now, you will be able to speak with them. Ask them for their name, ask them questions, for guidance, and they will easily give you the answers. I will come back to collect you in a short while."

Starlight tuned out the lady's voice as she drifted toward the shore of the lake. There, at the water's edge, was not an Angel, but her beloved.

"Gold," she whispered. When he turned and saw her there, his eyes lit up and he reached out for her. The tenuous link through the meditation meant that she had to imagine his touch, but she was grateful for the connection.

"My beautiful Starlight, I had hoped you would come."

Starlight smiled. "Have you missed me?"

"You know I have. Time passes so slowly it feels as

though every moment is an eternity."

"Which in fact it is, seeing as all of time is an illusion, and all that exists is this moment."

Gold smiled. "Indeed."

They sat on the pebbled beach, and ignored the glassy surface of the lake, preferring to gaze into each other's eyes instead.

"What is it like? Being on Earth?"

Starlight thought for a moment. "It's different. I knew what to expect, but I don't think I was quite prepared for the heaviness of the body. It takes conscious effort for me to retain my higher energy."

Gold sighed. "If even you find it difficult to vibrate at a higher level while on Earth, I cannot imagine how hard other Earth Angels must find it."

Starlight covered his weathered hand with her own slender one, imagining the feel of his skin against hers. "Sweet Gold, do not trouble yourself with the difficulties we face on Earth, focus instead on the beautiful missions we have gone there to accomplish."

"I know you are right," Gold whispered. "But the pain of being so far from your light has caused me to dwell on the darkness."

Starlight had no words to offer him, as she felt his pain as deeply as her own. She leaned toward him, and just as their lips were about to meet, a voice intruded.

"Say goodbye to your Angel, knowing that they are watching over you always, and that you can call on them whenever you need to."

She felt herself drifting backward, away from Gold, whose eyes were still closed in anticipation of the kiss. "I will see you again soon, my love," she whispered, as she left the Angelic Realm, and found herself back in the mists.

"I'm going to count up to ten, and when I reach ten, you will be fully back in your body, and grounded on Earth again."

Starlight was aware, as the lady brought them back again, of the tears falling down her cheeks, soaking into her blouse. When she finally opened her eyes, she saw that the lady leading the meditation was staring at her intently. One by one, the rest of the group shared their experiences, of meeting their Angels, and what their Angel told them. But Starlight didn't join in.

When the others had left, Starlight remained on her cushion, feeling a strong need to speak with the lady whose name was Maggie.

"Who are you, Angel?" Maggie asked her.

"My name is Star-Sarah," Starlight replied, correcting herself, but not before Maggie recognised her.

"Starlight?" she whispered, her hand to her mouth.

Starlight nodded, curious now, as to who Maggie was. "And who are you?"

Maggie smiled. "A friend of Velvet's. My name is Magenta."

Starlight's eyes widened. "Magenta! Velvet's friend, the Seer?"

"The one and the same." Maggie shook her head. "How are you here, Angel? Are you just visiting? Surely you cannot be an Earth Angel now?"

"I have come to Earth, yes, though not in the traditional way. I sensed that it was necessary for me to be here to help Velvet and the other Earth Angels. And the Children, of course."

"That's incredible. Have you made contact with Velvet yet? Or Violet, as she is now known?"

Starlight shook her head. "I arrived last week, I have been getting myself settled and decided to just follow my intuition, which led me here today. Do you live here?"

"No, I travel around doing these meditations in different healing centres, this is the first time I have done it here. Clearly, I was listening to my intuition too, because this is not one of my usual spots."

"Of course, I would expect nothing different of an Earth Angel such as yourself."

"So you believe the Golden Age is a possibility still? That we have another chance at this?"

"You saw the other ending?" Starlight asked, intrigued to see how much Maggie remembered.

"Yes, myself and many other Earth Angels have experienced a twenty-year vision, where we lost Velvet, and despite our best efforts, we also lost hope, and the world ended in darkness. It has changed my perspective and view of life, and I think it has transformed many other souls too."

"That is perfect. I knew that the soul would retain the memory of those twenty years, but I was unsure as to how much would consciously surface in each being."

"So they happened? Those twenty years were a memory, not a premonition?"

Starlight shifted on the cushion, suddenly uncomfortable in her human body. "Yes, they happened. Velvet came home to the stars, to me, and after twenty years of valiant effort on the part of the Earth Angels, the Golden Age still did not appear, the Rainbows did not arrive, and the world did indeed end in darkness."

Maggie gasped, her hand over her mouth. "I knew the vision felt too real, too vivid. And despite knowing that Violet did in fact try to leave us, I had hoped I was wrong. But how have things changed so dramatically this time around? I mean, Laguz and Velvet are now together, and other Flames are now finding each other, which is not what happened in the other time-line. What changed?"

"Velvet realised she had made a mistake. She realised she had to be here. Whether she got to be with Laguz or not, she was needed, she was a necessary part of the puzzle."

"That's it? Velvet's decision to return changed everything?"

"Yes."

"Wow."

There was a knock on the wall and both women looked up. The lady from the front desk was there. "I'm sorry to interrupt, but I have a therapist arriving soon with afternoon sessions booked, so I'm afraid I need to turf you out."

Maggie nodded. "Apologies, we got carried away." She and Starlight tidied away the cushions, gathered their things, and left the shop together, stepping out into the early afternoon sunlight. "Would you like to find a café somewhere, and continue this conversation? I feel like it's important that we talk right now, and not allow ourselves to slip back into human reality and become drawn away from the purpose at hand."

Starlight nodded. "I would like that very much. Do you know somewhere good?"

Maggie hitched her bag onto her shoulder. "I know the perfect place, it's just around the corner."

"Excellent, lead the way."

*   *   *

Her three days in Paris had been fun, but Leona hadn't seen any sign of her Flame, and so decided it was time to move on. She'd received an email from Greg to say that he and Violet had decided to continue travelling. They were going to travel around the UK first, visiting Violet's family, and then they would be heading back to France. Though Leona wanted to see them both again, she decided to head to Spain, to see if the cities there matched her vision.

Rucksack packed, Leona thanked her host, then headed for the Gare du Nord. She shook her head to herself as she walked along, wondering why she felt so possessed by the idea of seeking her Flame. Up until a few days before, she had been very happily single, with no desire to search all the cities of the world for the one who completed her.

But now she felt possessed by the need to see her. To touch her. To smell her sweet scent. In her vision, they did not meet for many years yet, but Leona was not happy to wait. She needed to meet her now.

When she reached the station, she found that the next train wasn't leaving for another hour. With a sigh, she headed for the nearest café, deciding to have a last cup of French hot chocolate before getting her ticket and moving on. She found a tiny table and dumped her rucksack down. Within moments of sitting down, the waitress approached her. She ordered the drink in her still very poor French, then got her notebook out of her rucksack, and flicked through it, reading snippets of her recent visions, looking at her sketches of what she had seen.

"Excusez-moi, puis-je rester ici se il vous plaît?"

Leona looked up and dropped her pen. The woman from her vision stood before her. Everything was as she remembered – beautiful red hair, green eyes and a wide smile. Leona nodded, and the woman sat opposite her, setting her bag down and then signalling to the waitress to order. She made her order in perfect French, while Leona watched, her mouth slightly open. Finally, when she had collected herself, she tried to speak to her.

"Er, il est belle, um journée, uhhh, aujourd'hui?"

The woman looked at her and smiled. "You're not French, I take it?"

Leona clocked the Australian accent this time and sighed in relief. "Oh good, you speak English. You know, I've been in France for quite a long time now, yet my French has still yet to improve."

The woman laughed. "I have been living here for five years, and only now do I feel confident enough to ask for the right thing, and not embarrass myself. It comes with practice." She noticed the baggage around Leona's feet. "Though it looks like you are leaving Paris?"

Leona blinked, and suddenly felt bereft at the thought of

leaving now. "Um, well, that was the plan, I was heading to Barcelona, but I got the wrong time for the train and just missed the last one."

"Time to try out your Spanish skills instead?" the woman teased.

Leona smiled. "I hadn't even thought about that, it's probably not the best idea, trying to learn yet another language badly."

"What awaits you in Spain?" Before Leona could answer, the woman shook her head. "I'm sorry, I'm being really very nosy, you don't have to answer that."

"No it's okay, I don't mind. To be honest, nothing. There is no reason for me to go to Spain, except-" Leona cut herself off mid-sentence, and a second later the waitress arrived with their orders. Leona hoped that the distraction would stop the woman from noticing her pause, but it didn't.

"Except?" she asked, taking a sip of her tea.

Leona sipped her hot chocolate in an attempt to stall, wondering what she should say. How could she admit that she was going to Spain simply to search for her? And now that she was sat in front of her, there was no reason for her to leave?

Despite knowing all of her life that she wasn't attracted to the opposite sex, Leona had never actually admitted it to anyone. She'd had a couple of boyfriends in school, just to fit in and go with the crowd, but it always felt so uncomfortable. She had never asked a girl out, or tried to have a relationship with another female, and despite being on a mission to find her, Leona hadn't actually planned what she would do once she had found her Twin Flame.

She blinked and realised that a couple of minutes had passed, and the woman was simply studying her, while drinking her tea and nibbling at a croissant. "Except nothing. There isn't any reason to go to Spain, I just hoped I might find something there."

The woman was quiet for a little longer, then appeared to

have decided something. She wiped her buttery hands on a napkin, then held her hand out to Leona. "I'm Reece."

Leona shook her hand, and wasn't surprised when her fingers tingled at Reece's warm touch. "I'm Leona," she replied.

After holding her hand for a few moments longer, Reece let go and finished the last of her tea. "So, Leona. Are you still going to Barcelona?" She nodded toward the clock. "The next train leaves in twenty minutes."

Without thinking about it too much, Leona shook her head. "No, I think might stay in Paris a while longer."

"Do you have someone you can stay with?"

"No, I've been HelpX'ing mostly, but I could-"

Reece stood up, leaving enough money on the table to cover both of their bills. "Come with me, I have somewhere you can stay."

Leona nodded and finished her hot chocolate. She stood as well and picked up her rucksack off the floor, before following her Flame out of the station and into the sunshine.

Chapter Five

"I'm so sorry about my mother," Violet apologised for the hundredth time. "She's been like that since I was a teenager, it's embarrassing, I'm so sorry."

Greg chuckled. "It's fine, honestly, I must admit, I was a little shocked when she started flirting with me, especially in front of your dad, but she didn't get too crazy, so it's okay."

Violet groaned and leaned her head back against the headrest. "I just wish she could behave herself! She's in her fifties, for crying out loud."

"I thought she was lovely," Greg said. "You wouldn't know she was that old."

"Oh, please don't let her hear you say that, she will be all over you even more."

Greg laughed and let the subject drop. "So now I've passed the parent test, are you ready to get out of here?"

Violet smiled. "I think I am. Shall we head to the tunnel?"

"Best idea you've had all day, after leaving your parents' house early, that is."

Violet laughed this time. "Yes, they were getting to be too much. Let's leave the country, immediately."

Greg concentrated on the road for a few moments as he navigated the busy traffic, and once they were on the motorway, he rested his hand on her knee.

Violet put the radio on, and after a few seconds she

switched it off abruptly, making him glance across at her.

"You okay?"

She sighed. "Yes." She leaned over and put the radio back on, and in silence, they listened to the song, the words piercing the air between them. Greg realised from the lyrics why she had reacted that way. The song hit very close to home. He pretended not to notice when she wiped her eyes with her sleeve, and chose to reach for her hand instead.

"I'm sorry," he said. "I don't expect everything to be forgotten immediately, as if the last few months never happened. I know what I did was awful, and that I hurt you so much," his voice broke, making Violet's tears flow faster. "I wish I could take it back, it was never my intention to do that."

Violet shook her head. "I know. And I also know that it was meant to happen that way. That we needed to experience that separation, otherwise this wouldn't be possible right now. I just hope that we don't have to go through that again."

"Me too," Greg agreed. "I could happily live the whole rest of my life without experiencing the loss of you again."

Violet smiled, and wiped her cheeks again with her sleeve. "It's good to hear you say that."

They listened to the radio for the rest of the journey. The light faded as they drove south, and night had fallen by the time they reached the tunnel. Greg looked over to see that Violet had fallen asleep, and he smiled. She always dozed off on long journeys. Their conversation earlier had bothered him, and something was nagging at the back of his mind, something that made him feel like he wouldn't be able to keep his word. That he wouldn't be able to avoid leaving her again. And that nagging feeling made him feel sick in the pit of his stomach.

A distant, half-forgotten memory of visiting Violet's gravestone resurfaced in his mind, and his heart thudded painfully against his ribs. He wished Leona was there. He wished he could ask her what she thought, whether she had Seen anything of the future that could help him.

He paid for the ticket and drove onto the train, and then gently nudged Violet awake. She allowed him to guide her into the back of the camper van, and then lay beside her on the small double bed, stroking her head gently. He touched the worn wooden pendant around her neck, then he took in every detail of her face, memorising every crease, every freckle. He noticed a tiny white scar on her forehead, and wondered how she'd got it. He wanted to know every last detail, everything about her life, who she was, inside and out.

Even if he had a hundred years with her, he didn't feel like it would be enough to know everything about her. And that made him feel sad. But he wouldn't allow himself to become swallowed up by that feeling. Instead he closed his eyes, breathed in her scent, and drifted off to sleep to the sound of the train.

*　　　*　　　*

"You have come at the perfect time!" Aria exclaimed to her tour group. "Just two days ago, this amazing Atlas moth hatched out of its cocoon. Though it's not a butterfly, and not quite so pretty, its size makes it pretty special."

The tour group, a mixture of people all different ages stared up in awe at the giant moth hanging from the ceiling.

"They can be up to twelve inches wide, and they have no mouths. Which is kind of sad, because once they hatch out, they live off of their body fat until they die. They will only last a week or two." Aria couldn't help the note of sadness in her voice, as she watched the magnificent creature. She had never encountered an Atlas moth when she was a Faerie, as they were not native to her part of the Elemental Realm. She wondered how they spoke or made friends when they had no mouths.

"Are they native to the UK?" one of the group asked.

Aria shook her head. "No, they are normally found in

Southeast Asia." Aria continued answering their questions, and then looked up to see Tim watching her. She smiled at him and waved, and he smiled back.

She finished the tour, and said goodbye to the group, happy that she had given them enough information on all the butterflies without bombarding them completely.

"I knew I was right," Tim said as she approached him.

"About what?"

"That you are a complete natural at this." He waved at their surroundings. "You fit right in here, it's like you are completely at home."

Aria smiled, blushing a little at the compliment. She shrugged. "I am at home here, that's why."

"Are you heading straight home after your shift? Or do you fancy going for a drink?"

Aria frowned. "Are you asking me out?" she asked, without thinking her words through first. Tim laughed and she felt a bit silly.

"As much as I wish I were, I think it would complicate things a little, don't you? Besides, I thought you were waiting to find Linen."

Aria's heart leapt at the mention of Linen's name. She had been keeping an eye out for him every day, but had yet to glimpse his face. Though she wasn't even sure what his face would look like, as she couldn't remember what body he had chosen to walk into. Surely she would recognise him though? As all these thoughts swirled around in her mind, Tim waited patiently for her to notice he was still there.

"How about a drink then?"

"Okay. Only as long as you promise not to hit on me. Because I am waiting for Linen."

Tim chuckled again. "If there's one thing I can say for Faeries, it's that they are unfailingly honest."

"There's a lot more you can say about Faeries than that," Aria argued.

"I'm sure there is."

They bantered all the way to the pub, and only paused briefly while ordering the drinks. Once settled, drinks in front of them, Aria looked around. "This is a nice place, do you come here much?"

"Occasionally. I don't drink much, but I thought we should celebrate your first week in your new job. You really are very good at it."

Aria beamed with pleasure. "I love it. I still can't quite believe that you gave me the job because you saw me dancing barefoot in the park, or that you are the alien that I shared a room with in the Fifth Dimension, but I do love how everything is going according to plan."

Tim laughed. "It sounds incredibly bizarre when you put it all that way, but somehow it makes perfect sense."

Aria sipped her drink then made a face. "What is this?"

"It's vodka and lemonade. If you don't like it, I'll get you something else."

Aria took another sip then shook her head. "No, it's okay, I just didn't know what to expect. I don't think I've ever had any alcohol except the time we tried to make our own berry wine in the Elemental Realm." She shook her head. "It really didn't taste good."

Tim chuckled. "Do you remember everything from being a Faerie and at the Academy? My memories aren't absolutely complete, just short snippets and the odd dream."

"Yes I do! It's amazing. I was so worried I would forget everything, which is why I didn't want to become human, but I remember it all. Especially Linen," Aria's face fell. "But what if I don't find him?"

Before Tim could reply, the first few notes of piano music drifted toward them and Aria's head snapped toward the sound.

"I'm sure-"

"Shh!" Aria hushed him. She held her hand up and

listened hard. The music continued and her heart leapt. "Linen!" she whispered. Without another thought, she got up from the table and went to find the source. When she found the piano tucked away in the corner, and she saw the person playing, her heart was thudding so loudly she could barely hear the notes over it. She would have recognised her song anywhere. She waited until he finished playing, not wanting to interrupt. When the last notes faded away, she couldn't stop herself from clapping loudly. So loudly, that he turned away from the piano toward her.

"Thank you," he said with a smile. He turned back to the piano and started to play another song. Aria frowned and her heart stalled. Didn't he know it was her?

"Linen?" she said over the music, going to his side. He continued playing but looked sideways at her.

"Sorry?"

"Linen, you are Linen," she said, aware that she might sound a little crazy, yet not caring.

He shook his head. "Sorry, you've got the wrong person."

"But you were playing my song," Aria insisted. "The song you wrote for me. Don't you remember?"

He continued playing, a frown on his face, but after a few moments he shook his head again. "I'm sorry, but I think you have the wrong person."

"Linen, it's Aria! I'm your Twin Flame, how can you not recognise me? Look at me!" Aria slammed down the piano cover, nearly taking his fingers off in the process.

"Hey! What the hell do you think you're doing?" He stood up, and towered over her. "I don't know who you are, or who Linen is, but I think you need to leave."

"I don't understand! I remember everything, you were supposed to as well! We came back to Earth, from the Other Side, just a couple of weeks ago, don't you remember?"

"Aria." Aria felt the hand on her arm, but she ignored it, stepping closer to the pianist.

"Linen, it's me, Aria. I know I don't have wings anymore, but it's still me!"

"Aria, I think we should leave, and perhaps come back to talk another time?" Tim was more insistent this time, and took her elbow to guide her away. She was oblivious to the crowd that had gathered, and the bouncer hovering nearby, ready to throw her out at the pianist's word.

"I'm not Linen, and you're crazy," he said. "Please leave now."

Aria's eyes welled up with tears, and she didn't try to resist as Tim led her out of the pub. The crowd parted to let them through, and she didn't even hear the mutters about her being a crazy lunatic. All she was aware of was her heart breaking into a million pieces.

Outside, Aria shivered violently in the chilly evening air. Tim pulled his jacket off and draped it over her shoulders, before wrapping his arm around her protectively and walking her toward the home that they now shared.

When they arrived back, he led her to her room, and helped her into bed. She was unresponsive to his questions, her eyes wide and staring.

"Aria," he said gently, trying one last time. "It'll be okay, he will remember, he will."

Aria closed her eyes, and a tear trickled down her cheek. Tim smoothed it away, pulled the covers up tight, and kissed her on the forehead.

"Goodnight, Faerie."

*   *   *

"There's something I need to say to you, but I don't know how to."

Ceri looked up at Charlie from her book and frowned at the serious tone of his voice. She set her book aside, not bothering to place her bookmark inside. "What is it?"

Charlie sat next to her on the sofa, and took her hands in his. "I know we've only known each other a very short time, but from the moment I first saw you, I knew we had met before, and for whatever reason, we never got a chance to be together. I don't want that to happen again, so," he took a deep breath, and Ceri found herself doing the same.

"Will you marry me?"

Ceri was speechless. She searched his face for a hint of it being a joke, but found none. He was completely serious, and from the slight dampness of his hands, she could tell he was really very nervous. She was silent for a moment, her mind whirling. It was all happening so quickly, was this really the best thing to do? But she knew, deep in her heart, that he was right. This was the first time they'd had a chance to be together, and they needed to make sure they made the most of it.

Before she could allow her more logical, practical side take over the situation, she smiled at the very nervous man at her side, and nodded. "Yes, I will."

He smiled, then leaned forward to kiss her. "You have no idea how afraid I was that you would say no."

"Actually, I think I have some idea," Ceri said, squeezing his hand. "We're connected, remember?"

"Of course. So how about a trip into town?"

"For what?"

Charlie shook his head. "A ring, of course. I wanted you to choose one that you liked, I know our tastes in jewellery are very different, and I didn't want to get it wrong."

Ceri laughed, and looked at his spiky wrist cuff compared to the delicate silver bracelet that adorned her small wrist. "I appreciate that. But we don't need to get a ring immediately, I don't mind waiting a while, I know that money is-"

Charlie put his finger to her lips. "Shh, I have the money put aside for this. It's important to me, that you have something that symbolises my commitment."

Ceri was surprised, she hadn't seen this side of him before. "Okay," she got up from the sofa. "Give me five minutes to get ready."

Charlie nodded, then waited patiently for his new fiancée to return.

*   *   *

"Here you are again."

Gold looked up at the concerned Angel, and nodded. "I cannot keep away, it is like an addiction I am unable break. I have left an Indigo Child in my place in the mists, which seems irresponsible, I know."

"You miss her, that's a natural thing. And there is no irresponsibility, the Indigo Child will easily manage." Pearl settled herself next to the lost Old Soul, who was absentmindedly playing with the rune necklace he now wore, and looked into the still lake, where she saw the beautiful face of Starlight. "She will be back sooner than you know."

"It doesn't seem to matter. Every nanosecond that she is not here, I feel it so strongly. Even though we were not in each other's pockets before, when she was in the heavens she felt much closer to me here. Earth feels so very far away."

"She has visited you though?"

"Yes, she appeared here, during what I can only imagine was a visualisation of sorts. But she wasn't really here, I could see her, hear her, but not feel her touch." He looked at Pearl, a tear hanging from his lashes. "I miss her touch the most."

Pearl put her arm around him. "Oh, Gold, there are no words of wisdom that I have to offer that will make the slightest bit of difference to the sorrow you feel, all I can say is, our Flames are with us, always. Wherever we or they may be."

"Where is your Flame, Pearl?"

Pearl smiled, and waved her hand across the lake,

changing the scene from Starlight to a grey haired male on Earth, who was busy writing. "You know where my Flame is, Gold. And you know that we have spent much of our existences apart. But we still hold each other in our hearts, in our souls." She turned to Gold. "Close your eyes, and feel her within you. She is in your heart. Feel her there, sense the unconditional, all-encompassing love she has for you."

Gold complied, and closed his eyes. He reached within and smiled when he sensed the bright twinkling lights of her soul dancing about. "She's here," he whispered. "I can feel her."

"Tell her you love her, and that you are there, within her whenever she needs you. Now walk away from this lake, and return to your duties. Fill your time with helping souls cross to the hereafter, and before you know it, she will be home with you again."

As much as her words pained him, Gold knew that Pearl was right. "I love you," he whispered to the twinkling lights. He sensed their acknowledgement, then without opening his eyes, he stood, and walked back toward the gates, leaving Pearl sat on the edge of the lake, watching her own Flame from afar.

*   *   *

"Is this really happening?"

Reece smiled at Leona, and reached out to stroke her face. "Yes, it really is."

Leona bit her lip. "I've never done this before, I mean, it's all so fast…"

"Shh," Reece pressed her finger to Leona's lips, then shifted closer to her and kissed her softly. "It's perfect," she whispered. "I had no reason to be in the station yesterday, no reason at all. I just felt pulled there, and then when I got there, I desperately needed a cup of tea, and the seat opposite you was the only space available. And then when I saw you…" her smile grew wider. "I knew you. I knew I needed to speak to you. It was as though you were my dear friend I was meeting again after a very long time, but there was something else too, a passion, a yearning, that I don't think I have ever felt before."

Leona nodded to everything Reece said, knowing that she felt the same way. But even with the depth of her feelings, it was difficult to believe that within hours of meeting, they had fallen into bed together, and shared an intensely passionate night together.

"I've never been with a woman before," Leona whispered. "I've never even admitted how I felt, to anyone."

"It's not easy," Reece said. "It's taken me a long time to be comfortable in my own skin. I never really felt like I fit in on this planet, and then, to find that I had no interest in men, well, my family despaired of me." She chuckled. "They thought I was so weird. My mum tried everything to make me fit in, and to fulfil her hopes, her dreams, but it didn't work out. So I left Australia and travelled. I had been travelling for eight months when I ended up in Paris, and somehow, I felt like I had come home. And that there was a reason I was here." She leaned forward to kiss Leona again. "And finally, I think I know what the reason is."

"Do you have any contact with your family now?" Leona asked, thinking of her own family back in the UK, who she had barely contacted since leaving on her travels.

"Not really. I check in with my mum once every few months, just so they know I'm still okay. But we never really have much to say to each other. I do really feel that our true family is made up of the people who understand us, on a soul level, not the ones who happen to have the same blood running through their veins."

"I couldn't agree more. I met a guy while travelling, who I knew from another life. Spending time with him was like having a big brother, and it was amazing. All of my siblings are a lot younger than me."

"Aren't younger siblings irritating?" Reece laughed. "I have two younger brothers, and an older sister. As a child I just hid away from my brothers, they were so horrible to me. I was the only one in my family with red hair, so they used to tease me, and say I was adopted."

"That's horrible!"

Reece laughed again. "I even checked my birth certificate, just to be sure. In all honesty, I used to wish that I were adopted, because then that would explain why I didn't fit into my family."

"It's probably because you're an Earth Angel. None of us feel like we fit in."

Reece frowned, and suddenly pushed herself up into a sitting position. "An Earth Angel?"

Leona sat up too, and she rested her hand on Reece's leg, suddenly feeling bold. "Yes, in your past life, you were not human. You were from another realm, and you are only human now, so that you could help with the Spiritual Awakening."

Reece shook her head. "How do you know this? I've never heard of that before. Another realm? What do you mean?"

Leona smiled. "It's a lot to take in, shall we get something to eat before I try to explain? I have a book you can read if you want."

"Sure, let's grab some food." Reece turned to get out of bed, but then changed her mind and slid back toward Leona. She leaned in to kiss her, then pulled her down back under the covers.

Leona kissed her back. Then she murmured, "I guess food can wait a few minutes."

Chapter Six

Violet sat on the damp sand, the moisture seeping into the fabric of her jeans. The wind whipped through her long hair, and she cringed at the thought of having to brush it later. But for now, she enjoyed the salty air, and the feeling of the sea spray misting her skin. Somehow, everything became balanced again, when she sat by the sea. The sound of the waves roaring in, the sound of the gulls calling to each other, the wind rushing past her. It was calming.

And she needed the calm that morning. She had woken up in Greg's arms, after having had the same recurring dream she'd had months before, when he had broken up with her and broken her heart.

After waking up so suddenly, it had taken several minutes to calm her heartbeat down. Greg had been sound asleep, oblivious to the terror she felt, not only because she had been drowning, but because of the overwhelming feeling of déjà vu.

She had slipped out of bed, put on some warm clothes, and grabbed her diary before sneaking out of the van, and down to the beach. As she'd walked the short distance, her leg ached, reminding her of the other time she had drowned, and had been saved by Greg.

Violet pulled her diary out of her pocket, and flipped through the pages to the day she tried to leave Earth and go home.

I know that I died today. I know that this is a second chance, and one that I am very lucky to have. When I died, I went home, to my true home, to the stars, and I was with my sister, Starlight. Together, we watched Earth, and over the course of twenty years, despite the efforts of the Earth Angels, it did not Awaken on a mass scale.

So when the world was about to end, I chose to come back. I asked Gold if I could return to this point, return to my life, and to have a second chance to fulfil my mission on this planet. Because despite the heartbreak I felt when Greg pushed me away, I know that my mission is not to be with him. I know that my purpose is not living a long life with my Flame, but to Awaken the world, so it does not head for the same fate that I watched from the stars. So here I am, alive again, after being among the stars for twenty years, happy to continue my mission, despite being assured that I will not get to be with Greg.

And that's okay. I have made peace with that. Instead of drowning in the sorrow of missing his touch, I must live every moment as fully as possible.

Violet looked up from her diary at the waves, and sighed. She and Greg were never meant to get back together. Was that why she was having the reoccurring drowning dream again? Because they were somehow breaking a universal law? She didn't believe that they would be together in that moment if the universe did not want them to be together, but how could Gold be wrong? It didn't make sense. Was it possible for her to fulfil her mission with Greg by her side? Or would they be parted again?

"Hey."

She closed her diary and looked up to see Greg making his way toward her. "I was worried when I woke up and you were gone. Are you okay?"

She nodded as he sat beside her, wrapped his arm around her and leaned in for a kiss. When their lips met, she felt a tingle through her body all the way to her toes. She lingered in his kiss for a long time, and when they finally pulled apart, he searched her face.

"What is it?" he asked.

Somehow they were now so sensitive to each other's energies, that she couldn't hide anything from him.

"Bad dreams," she whispered.

His eyes widened as he understood the full meaning of what she was saying. "Drowning?"

She sighed. "I'm sure it doesn't mean anything."

Greg was quiet for a while, watching the waves. "Did you get those dreams when we were apart?"

Violet frowned. "No, but what has that got to do with anything?"

Greg didn't answer her. He watched the waves for a few minutes longer, then looked into her eyes and held her gaze. "Do you sometimes feel like we shouldn't be together?"

Violet's breath caught. Despite thinking the same thing just moments before, hearing him say the words was like a slap in the face. "Don't do this," she whispered, her heart now hammering in her chest. "Don't push me away. You said you would never do that again."

Greg took hold of her hands. "And I meant it. I don't want to push you away, but I also can't get rid of this nagging feeling that somehow, we weren't meant to get back together. I mean," he shook his head in frustration, and closed his eyes. "Maybe it's just not the best thing for you, to be with me."

"How can you say that?" Violet pulled her hands away and stood up abruptly, her diary dropping to the sand. She ignored it and walked toward the shore. Her temper was rising and she needed to calm herself. She knew that getting angry wasn't going to help either of them, but she *was* angry. Angry that he was trying to break up with her, and angry that she felt, on some level, that he may be right to do so. That maybe he knew that Gold had said they wouldn't be together.

She stood at the water's edge for a minute before she felt him standing next to her. He held out her diary and she took it without a word.

"I love you. I love you with everything I have. But what if that's not enough? Or what if it's too much? I just feel like I'm stopping you from following your mission."

Violet turned to him, a frown on her face. "What if I don't care? What if I would rather be with you than following my mission?"

"I care. I know that you have so much to do, and I don't want to be the reason you aren't doing it."

"You're talking rubbish. If you don't want to be with me, then just say so. But don't make up some bullshit," Violet's voice broke, and she couldn't hold back her tears any longer. "Don't bullshit me just to push me away. Tell me the truth."

"I am," Greg said, his own voice filled with pain. "Let's not do this right now, let's go back to the van and have a cup of tea." He wrapped his arms around her and despite her anger, she melted into his embrace.

She allowed him to lead her back to the van, where he put the kettle on and she tucked her diary back into her drawer.

Once they had settled with steaming mugs of tea in hand, Violet felt a bit calmer.

"I'm so sorry that I keep hurting you," Greg said, his head on her shoulder. "I don't want to keep doing that. But I know that I cannot lie to you, that I cannot keep what I feel or think from you. And I was just trying to tell you how I felt. I'm not trying to push you away. I wish more than anything that I could push away this weird feeling, but I haven't managed to do it yet."

"I just know that I can't go through losing you again. I just can't. You don't understand what it did to me last time."

"I know, and I'm sorry. I wish I could take back all the pain I caused."

They were both quiet for a while. Violet sipped her

scalding tea, her mind reeling. She wished she hadn't shared her dream now, then this conversation wouldn't have happened. But it was true what he'd said; they could no longer hide anything from each other. And though she loved the barrier-less transparency, it scared her. Sometimes she wished they could be a regular couple, unawake and unaware of the bigger picture, just content to be in each other's company.

"I love you, Violet. And I will stay with you for as long as it makes sense for both of us."

His words stabbed her through the heart. Because they held the promise that sometime soon, being together would no longer make sense.

*　　　*　　　*

"Aria, please come and eat something. I'm worried about you."

Aria didn't move from her place in bed, and in fact she had only left her room to use the bathroom and get drinks for the last three days. "I'm not hungry," she said, her voice devoid of emotion.

Tim sighed. "I'm afraid I'm not going to take no for an answer. So I'm going to stand here and bug you until you finally join me." When she still didn't move, he changed tack.

"I hate eating by myself. Until you moved in, I hadn't realised just how lonely and boring it is. Please don't make me eat in front of the TV and force me to watch soap operas."

Aria sighed. "Okay." She slowly pulled the covers back, and got out of bed, pulling one of Tim's old jumpers over the top of her pyjamas. She followed him to the dining table, and sat down. Despite her words, her stomach growled when she smelled the food. Tim really was a very good cook. She waited until he had sat down and started eating before she started to do the same.

She had finished half her meal when she felt Tim's gaze

on her. She looked up and gave him a tiny smile. "It's very tasty, thank you. I'm sorry I've been such a grumpy Faerie."

Tim sighed. "Oh, Aria, it's totally understandable. I know that you are hurting right now, but just because he didn't remember straight away, doesn't mean you have to give up. It just might mean that perhaps you should get to know him in a more human way."

Aria frowned. "What do you mean by that?"

"I mean that instead of talking about other dimensions, other lives and Twin Flames, perhaps you should approach him as a person. Talk about his music, about your work, about normal, everyday things. Show him that you're not a crazy psychopath. Let him get to know you. Then as time goes on, he may just remember."

Despite her reservations about trying to be a normal human, Aria's heart lifted at the idea that Linen might remember. "Do you think it's possible?"

"I think anything is possible."

They finished their meal in silence, and Aria was glad for the quiet, because her mind was whirling with ideas on how to appear normal.

"Would you like some chocolate pudding for dessert? We could watch a movie if you want to join me."

Aria smiled, feeling genuinely happy for the first time in days. "I would love some chocolate pudding. What movie can we watch?"

They took their dishes to the kitchen, and Tim served them chocolate pudding and ice cream. "There's a movie about aliens on TV tonight, I haven't watched it before, but it might be good."

"An alien movie? Okay, I guess. But next time we'll have to watch a Faerie one, just so it's even."

Tim chuckled as they settled onto the sofa. "Deal."

*   *   *

"I hate that we don't have our own space," Ceri whispered as they snuck past Charlie's mother's bedroom door after going for a walk.

Once they were safely in his room, he pulled her close and kissed her. "I know, but neither of us can afford to rent right now, so what other option do we have? At least here, no one will bother us," he said, referring to the fact that Ceri had four younger siblings who also all lived at home, and could be counted on to burst in on them at the most inappropriate moment.

"I guess, but it's hardly comfortable, squishing into your single bed."

Charlie sighed, and felt some anger bubbling to the surface. "What do you want me to do? I don't have the money right now."

"I told you we shouldn't have spent that money on my ring," Ceri said, twisting the simple band around her finger. "We should have been more practical, more thrifty. I don't really need anything to show that I'm yours."

"Yes, you do. We are not returning or selling your ring." Charlie swallowed his anger and his annoyance and pulled her in for a kiss. "Let's not think about it now, we will get our own place soon, I promise. But please, don't wish that we hadn't got the ring, it's important to me."

Ceri sighed. "Okay, I'm sorry. I love my ring, I do. I just want us to have our own space, that's all."

"I know, I do too." To stop any further communication, Charlie pulled her toward the single bed and lay her down on it, before showering her with kisses until she started to giggle, dissolving the tension.

Despite having only been together such a short time, Charlie couldn't believe how easily and how perfectly they fit together when they made love. Even though he had been so in love with Violet, it hadn't been as mind-blowing as this when they slept together. There hadn't been anywhere near the degree of passion and intensity that existed between himself and Ceri. He pulled himself out of his thoughts and focused on the sensations of the moment, as his body entangled with hers, and when they climaxed together, all thought of Violet was driven out of his mind.

"Charlie?"

"Mmmhmm?" Charlie was drifting into unconsciousness when Ceri's voice pulled him back to reality.

"Is this her?"

Charlie's eyes flew open to see Ceri holding his metal box and the photo of Violet from within it. "How did you find that?" he demanded, grabbing the photo from her hand, feeling violated and angry suddenly.

"It fell out while we were making love." Ceri smiled. "It's okay, I know that you loved her a lot, I'm not jealous that you still have her photo. She's really beautiful."

Charlie's anger simmered, and he looked down at the photo, creased from his sudden claiming of it. Why did he feel so angry when Ceri was being so understanding?

"Please don't go through my things," he said, putting the photo safely back into the box. He got up from the bed, and went over to his desk where he tucked the box away into a drawer. He turned back to see Ceri looking shocked. "Maybe you should go home tonight." He knew his tone was clipped and short, but he couldn't help it.

"I'm sorry," Ceri said, getting up too. She walked over to him, not bothering to cover herself up. She touched his arm. "I didn't mean to pry, honestly." She tried to smile, but Charlie could see that he had upset her. "I'll go home, I have to get up early for work anyway. See you tomorrow?"

Charlie didn't respond to her touch or her words, and while she got dressed and gathered her things, he went downstairs to make himself a drink. When she came down minutes later, she tried to kiss him goodnight, but her effort landed on his cheek instead.

"Goodnight, Charlie. I love you."

He heard the door close softly behind her, and then he couldn't keep it in any longer. He slammed his empty glass into the sink, shattering it. "Fuck!" he shouted, not caring that it was past midnight and that he would probably wake his mum and the neighbours.

Sure enough, he heard footsteps coming down the stairs seconds later.

"Charlie? What's going on?"

"Nothing, Mum. Go back to bed."

His mum stood in the doorway, surveying the scene. "Shall I clean it up?" she asked. Charlie hated the resigned tone in her voice, the one that he'd heard frequently before his Awakening.

"No. I'll do it."

"Okay, good night."

Charlie ignored her, and began the painstaking task of retrieving all of the tiny shards of glass out of the sink. Why did he still have so much anger within him? Ceri hadn't done anything wrong. She was curious, that's all. And she wasn't even angry that despite them being engaged, he still had his ex-girlfriend's photo next to his bed! She was the kindest, most understanding soul he had ever met, and they fit together perfectly. So why was he acting like such an asshole?

The tiny shards cut into his fingers as he cleaned up, but he didn't care. The pain of the tiny cuts eased his anger a little, and by the time he finished, he felt calm enough to apologise for his actions. He returned to his room, and retrieved his phone from where it was charging on his desk, then got into his cold bed. He picked out Ceri's number from his phone book and pressed the green button.

"Hello?" her whispered answer let him know that she was home safe, and that she was trying not to wake the house up.

"I love you. I'm sorry I snapped at you," he said.

He could almost hear her smile. "I love you too. It's okay, I just wish you would let me help you through those moments. There's no need to push me away. I love you no matter what you do or say."

Charlie sighed. "I think you may just be an Angel sent from heaven."

Ceri giggled softly. "No, not an Angel. Just a human who is madly in love with your beautiful soul. I better go, I don't want to wake everyone up. Good night, Charlie."

"Good night, Ceri."

* * *

"Sarah Light?"

Starlight looked up at her name being called, and she then followed the nurse to the doctor's office beyond the reception. The nurse knocked, then opened the door and waved her in. Starlight's nose wrinkled at the sterile smell that greeted her, and she went inside and perched on the hard chair that was offered.

"What can we do for you today?" the doctor asked, sounding bored.

"I've had headaches every day for a week now. I have tried painkillers, but they're not working. I tried meditation and alternative therapies, but they're not working either." She sighed. "It's hard for me to concentrate on anything and I have too much to do not to be able to concentrate."

"Have you had these headaches before this week?"

Starlight smiled a little, glad that he wasn't looking at her. How could she tell him that she hadn't been human before a couple of weeks before? "No, I haven't."

"So they're unusual? Out of the blue? But persistent?"

"Yes, they are. And they're painful. It's hard to see or do anything."

The doctor did a thorough examination, then made some

notes, a frown on his face.

"Have you had your eyes tested recently?"

"Yes, two days ago. They said my eyesight was perfectly fine, but if the headaches continued to see a doctor."

The doctor had a look on his computer and sighed. "I don't seem to have any of your previous medical notes, but I think perhaps you should have some further tests to rule out anything serious. I will refer you to the local hospital."

Starlight frowned. "Do you think it could be something serious?"

"It's hard to tell, but it's best to be safe. I will call the hospital now and see if they have any slots available this afternoon."

Starlight was surprised at the efficiency and urgency of his actions. She felt unfamiliar human emotions of panic creeping up on her, and she started to bite her thumbnail, something that she never imagined she would do.

She zoned out while the doctor spoke on the phone, only becoming aware of him again when he called her name a couple of times.

"They can fit you in at four this afternoon. Do you know where the hospital is?"

Starlight nodded, knowing that she could find out easily. She didn't want to stay in his office a second longer than necessary. She took the referral letter that he printed and signed, then left the surgery in a daze. She had assumed she would be leaving with a prescription for some stronger painkillers, not with a hospital appointment.

She spent the next couple of hours window shopping, though she saw little more than her own scared reflection in the glass. After asking a couple of people, she got directions to the hospital, and got the bus there for four o'clock. She went to the main reception, and they directed her to the right department. The energies in the hospital made her feel queasy as she walked through the corridors. She could feel the sadness and anger and horror of the people who were suffering within the rooms beyond. A couple of times, she nearly turned around and left, wondering why on earth she would subject herself to this. But the stabbing pain in her right temple made her continue; she really couldn't bear to put up with the headaches much longer.

After checking in at the reception desk, Starlight sat in the waiting room, and stared at the scary posters on the walls, talking about the symptoms of different diseases.

"Hey, are you okay?"

Starlight looked up to see a guy sitting next to her, a look of concern on his face. She realised then that she had been crying. She took the tissue he offered her, and wiped her eyes.

"Um, yes. Just a little scared."

He smiled, and Starlight noticed then how beautiful his eyes were. "Hospitals are a pretty scary places. Are you here for tests? Or results?"

"Tests," Starlight whispered. "I have no idea what to expect, I've never had to do anything like this before."

"I am sure you will be absolutely fine. I've been through loads of tests, and so far, they can't figure out what's wrong with me, but hey, I'm still here." He smiled. "My name is Gareth, what's yours?"

"Sarah." Starlight smiled back and offered her hand to him, and he shook it. "Why are you having tests?"

"Migraines. Been going on for weeks now."

"I've had bad headaches for a week," Starlight said. "I thought the doctor would just give me some painkillers, not send me to hospital."

"I'm sure it's just a precaution. Though I do wish they'd figure out what was causing mine."

Starlight frowned. "I hope they can figure it out for you. I've only had headaches for a week and they're already driving me crazy."

"I completely understand. My biggest problem is that I

haven't been able to concentrate on work. My company is being very understanding, giving me time off, but they can only do that for so long."

"Sarah Light?"

Starlight looked up at the nurse calling her name, and then looked at Gareth who nodded at her reassuringly. "Do you want to meet here afterward? We could go for a drink and compare headache notes."

Starlight smiled and nodded, then followed the nurse out of the waiting room.

*   *   *

"What is it?" Leona took Reece's hands and squeezed them. "Talk to me." The tears rolled down Reece's face, breaking Leona's heart.

"It's my mother, she's sick." Reece bit her lip. "I need to see her. I need to go home."

Leona pulled Reece into her arms and hugged her. "Oh, of course you do. I'll go with you."

Reece sobbed into Leona's jumper, and Leona's heart sank when she felt her shaking her head. "No, I need to go alone. They've never accepted the fact that I'm a lesbian, if I take you with me, it will just make the situation worse."

"I can just say I'm your friend, they don't have to know we're together, we don't have to tell them."

"They'll know." Reece stroked Leona's cheek. "They'd only have to see us standing beside each other to know that our feelings run so much deeper than just as friends."

Leona's heart began to race. "But I just found you. I can't lose you this soon, please, let me come with you."

"I don't want to leave you, but it just wouldn't work. I'm sorry. You can stay here in the apartment until I get back, though."

Leona sighed, walked over to the window, and looked out

at the Parisian skyline. "How long will you be gone?"

Reece followed her Flame, and wrapped her arms around her. "At least a couple of weeks. I don't know how long she has, but I need to be there for her."

Leona nodded. She didn't want to be selfish, but at the same time, the idea of letting Reece go, of her being so far away... it was almost too much to bear. She turned around to face Reece, and looked into her bright green eyes. "I'll miss you," she whispered.

More tears fell and Reece nodded. "I need to book my flight. I'm hoping to leave tomorrow at the latest."

"I'll help you pack," Leona said. Reece smiled and leaned in to kiss her.

The next twenty-four hours passed by in a blur of tears, kisses, and bad attempts to laugh. All Leona knew, was that when she found herself standing in Charles de Gaulle Airport, moments before she was about to say goodbye to her Flame for an undetermined amount of time, all she wanted to do was collapse into a heap and sob.

"I'll email you as soon as I get there," Reece said, her arms wrapped tightly around Leona. "I can't believe how hard this is. I'm so sorry that you can't come with me, I wish you could, but,"

Leona kissed her to silence her, unaware of the attention they were getting from fellow passengers waiting to go through security. "Shh," she said. "Focus on your mum, on seeing your family. I'll be here waiting for you when you get back."

Reece nodded, then released Leona, taking a step back. She smiled, and hitched her bag higher on her shoulder. "I love you," she said.

Leona's heart leapt at the words, it was the first time either of them had uttered them. She pulled Reece back for another kiss, then when they parted, she repeated the sentiment. She also realised in that moment, that it was the first time she had ever said the words to anyone.

When Reece finally pulled herself away and Leona watched her go through the security gate, she was suddenly thrown into a vision. The horror of the situation was immediately apparent as she looked around the inside of the plane. Passengers were screaming, oxygen masks were flailing around as the plane lurched sickeningly, and air stewardesses did their best to keep everyone calm, but the fear on their faces was unmistakable. Leona looked around to find herself face to face with Reece, who was ashen, her eyes closed tightly, as she prayed to God that she would live through it, and get to see Leona again. Seconds later, there was a deafening crash and the vision dissolved into flames.

"Noooo!" Leona screamed. She blinked rapidly, and ran toward the security gate that Reece had disappeared through. Before she could get any words out, she was instantly apprehended by several security guards. "Reece!" she screamed. "Come back! The plane is going to crash! Reece!" Her terror made her struggle against the men, and she found herself on the floor, being pinned down while they put handcuffs on her, and talked rapidly into their radios, calling for back up. But she didn't care about her own safety in that moment, she had to stop Reece from boarding the plane.

"Let me go!" she cried. "The plane is going to crash!"

But they weren't listening.

Chapter Seven

"Whoa now, slow down, I can't understand a word," Greg said, straining to hear Leona's voice filtering through. Violet frowned at him in concern, wondering what was going on.

"You're being held by police? At the airport? Okay, we're a couple of hours away, but we are heading straight to you. Have you got anyone there with you?"

Without being prompted, Violet pulled in the chairs and table from outside the van, where they were parked outside their HelpX host's house. Then she ran into the house to let them know they would have to leave immediately.

By the time she ran back out, Greg was behind the wheel with the engine running. Violet jumped into her seat next to him and put her seatbelt on. "What's going on?"

Greg shook his head. "The line was so bad, I couldn't make out everything she said, but basically, she's being held by airport security and the police at Charles de Gaulle Airport. I hope I heard her wrong, but it sounded like she said they thought she was a terrorist."

"What? Leona? A terrorist?" Violet laughed, but the look on Greg's face told her he wasn't joking. "Shit. How is that even possible?"

"I have no idea, all I know is she is completely freaked out. She was crying and saying something about her Flame."

"I didn't know she'd met her Flame?"

"Neither did I." He concentrated on navigating the narrow roads for a few minutes, then sighed. "I wish I had kept in better contact with her over the last couple of weeks. I really hope I can help her, she helped me so much over the last eighteen months."

Violet reached out to squeeze his knee. "I know. She'll be okay, we'll do everything we can to help her."

"Thank you." Greg returned the squeeze, then gripped the steering wheel with both hands, and forced the van to chug along a lot faster than felt comfortable for the old vehicle. Violet switched on the radio, to try and diffuse the tension a little. But by the time they reached the outskirts of Paris, Violet felt so tense, she couldn't wait to get out of the van to stretch. Greg navigated his way to the airport, following the signs for the last few miles. They pulled into the car park, then hand in hand, ran toward the main terminal.

It took a further fifteen minutes of Greg's broken French to find out where Leona was being held, then they were finally led down a maze of corridors to the interview room where she sat, huddled on a plastic chair. When the door opened and she saw them both, she jumped up, but couldn't go any further because the cuffs on her wrists were chained to the table.

"Leona!" Greg went to hug her but was stopped by the guard.

"Pas de contact!" he barked.

Greg stopped short and he and Violet were forced to sit on the other side of the table. "Lee, what's going on?"

Leona shook her head, her tear-stained face red and puffy. "I saw it, I saw the plane going down, and Reece was on it. I tried to call her back, but then the security thought I was a terrorist, because I kept saying the plane was going to crash."

Greg's eyes widened, and he saw the guards listening with interest. He could only assume that the mirror on the wall was two-way and that they were being closely listened to. He leaned toward her. "Did you explain? About your visions? Did the plane take off already?" He knew how accurate Leona was. If she saw the plane go down, then it would.

"I tried to, but they couldn't understand me. They thought I meant that I had been planning for it to go down, not that I saw it in a vision. They were going to get me a translator, but I said I wanted you instead. They won't tell me anything about the plane." She looked at Violet in horror. "Reece might still be on it, it might have taken off anyway."

Violet reached across to touch her hand in comfort, and the guard didn't stop her. "Is she your Flame?" she asked softly.

"Yes, we met just a week ago. Her mum is ill, in Australia, she's going home to see her."

Greg shook his head. "Shit. What can I do, Lee? We need to get an English-speaking lawyer, and we need to get you out of here. We also need to stop that plane from taking off, when was it supposed to leave?"

Leona glanced up at the clock. "Fifteen minutes ago," she whispered.

Greg nodded, then stood up. "I'll be right back," he muttered to Violet. He asked to leave the room, then asked the guard outside to speak to the person in charge.

"What is it?" the man asked.

"Are you in charge?" Greg asked, not bothering with niceties.

"I am Detective Chevalier. And you are?"

"I am worried that you might have allowed the plane to take off already. Do you understand what a psychic is?"

The detective frowned, and Greg searched his memory for a word in French that would help him, but he came up blank. "We need a translator, and fast. There are a lot of people who could be in a lot of danger right now, and you need to start listening."

Just then, a guard approached them, with a young man in tow. "Detective, est la traducteur."

The detective spoke rapidly to the young man, who then turned to Greg. "I am Pierre, what are you trying to convey to the Detective?"

As quickly as he could, Greg explained how Leona could see the future to the translator, who then did his best to relay the message to the detective. At first the man's face was sceptical and disbelieving, but as Greg relayed several stories of all the times Leona had been right, how someone she loved was on the flight, and she was just very scared for them; his features began to soften.

"Please, just tell me, has the flight taken off?" Greg asked again. He couldn't bear to have to tell Leona if it had in fact taken off already.

The detective was quiet for a moment, then he shook his head, and Greg sighed in relief. He spoke rapidly through the translator again.

"No, we have grounded the flight, and have conducted a thorough examination of the plane. The passengers are all safe."

"Thank you. Have you found anything wrong with the plane yet?"

The detective shook his head again and spoke through the translator. "We have not finished our tests yet, but I can assure you, the plane is not going anywhere right now." He was thoughtful for a moment. "Did she see anything in her 'vision' that could help us work out the problem?"

Though the translator was more diplomatic, Greg could hear the derision in the detective's words when he asked the question, but he chose to ignore it. "Uncuff her, let me tell her the plane hasn't taken off and that her friend is safe, then let me talk to her. She can't See anything when she's upset and stressed out."

After a moment of thought, the detective nodded, and the three men returned to the interview room.

Violet and Leona looked up, and Greg was relieved to see

that his friend looked a little less frightened. "Leona, the detective is going to uncuff you, so we can talk properly. They want your help – to work out what's wrong with the plane."

"Has it taken off?" Leona asked as the metal was removed from her wrists.

"No," Greg said. "They grounded it to examine it."

Leona collapsed into her chair in relief, and tears sprang to her eyes. "Reece is okay?"

"All of the passengers are still in the airport, they're all safe."

Once Leona was free, the detective left, taking the translator and the guard with him, leaving Greg and Violet to speak with Leona.

"Lee, they need your help, to work out why the plane might have crashed. They haven't said what they're going to do with you, but I get the feeling that if you can work it out, and they find the proof, they will believe you and let you go."

Leona shook her head. "How am I supposed to work it out? You know that my visions don't work like that, I just See what comes through, there's no real structure to them."

"Can you go into a meditation and focus your mind to that moment in time, try to tune into it somehow?" Violet asked.

Leona sighed. "I can try. To be honest, all that is in my mind right now is the thought that Reece is okay."

Greg smiled at her. "Yes, she is, and I promise I will do my best to make sure you can see her as soon as possible."

Leona nodded. "Okay then, I'll try to See something." She sat back in her chair and tried to relax. She closed her eyes and breathed deeply, trying to release all of the tension and fear that had consumed her for the previous few hours. After struggling to quiet her mind for a few minutes, she felt herself slipping out of the current reality, and into a vision.

"In Paris, a 747 bound for Australia was grounded today, on the advice of a psychic who claimed it was going to crash. Investigators found that the plane did in fact have a major fault in the starboard engine, which had been missed in the pre-flight checks. It has sparked an inquiry into the incident, and there have been further delays as other 747s have been checked for this fault before they have been allowed to take off. I'm now joined by Joseph Lachance, an aircraft engineer, who will explain to us exactly what the problem is…"

Leona opened her eyes, and relayed the vision to Greg and Violet. She asked for a pen and paper, which Violet scrambled in her handbag to find. Leona then sketched out as accurately as she could, what the fault was, as had been shown to her by the engineer. When she finished, she pushed it over to Greg.

He smiled at Leona, took the paper and left the room. Outside, he handed it to the detective. "This is the fault. Get the engineers to check it. Leona said they missed it in the pre-flight checks."

The detective took the paper, disbelief still evident in his face. He called someone on his radio, and explained the fault to them, then he listened to the response.

"We will find out soon. Until then, your friend must stay with us."

"Then we will stay with her," Greg responded. "Is there any way we can get some food and drink though? She must be starving by now."

The detective nodded to the guard and motioned for Greg to follow him. Greg followed him to the staff canteen, where he bought some bottles of water and some chocolate bars and various snacks. When he got back to the room, Violet and Leona were chatting away. It sounded like Leona was filling her in on how she had met Reece. They looked up when he entered, and Leona's eyes lit up at the sight of the chocolate.

They tucked into the snacks, and Greg suddenly realised how hungry he was too, so he joined them. After twenty minutes, the detective returned with the translator.

"They found the fault. Exactly as you described. They have assured me that there is no way you could have had anything to do with it, so I am letting you go."

Greg, Violet and Leona simultaneously sighed in relief.

"We apologise for any inconvenience caused, and we are thankful that you brought the matter to our attention."

"Can I see Reece? She should have been on the flight."

"Another plane was arranged for the Australian passengers, and that flight has already left."

Leona's face fell. "Oh, I see."

Greg reached across to grip her hand. "I'm sorry, Lee."

Leona shook her head. "It's okay. She'll be okay now, and besides, I don't want her to know what happened today. I don't want her to know what I saw." She looked up at the detective. "May I go now?"

He nodded, and the three friends got to their feet.

"We'll take you home," Greg said. Leona nodded, and they filed out of the room. Greg and Violet held hands, and Greg held out his other hand to Leona, who took it gratefully.

Once they got Leona's belongings back, they went out to the van, and the shock set in. Violet wrapped a blanket around Leona, who was shivering uncontrollably, and sat in the back of the van with her, trying to warm her up, while Greg drove them to Reece's apartment.

When they got there, Greg immediately started making hot drinks for them all, while Violet found a warm cardigan for Leona to put on. Leona slipped it over her clothes and breathed in the intoxicating scent of her Flame. "It all seems so unreal," she whispered.

Greg handed her the mug of hot chocolate, and she took it gratefully.

"Thank you, both of you, for coming to rescue me. I had no idea what to do, or who to call. If you hadn't been in the country, I don't know what I would have done."

"I hope you would have had the sense to ask for a lawyer. I can't believe they treated you like that. A terrorist! I can't imagine anyone who looks less like one than you."

Leona smiled. "If you could have seen me you may change your mind on that one. I was acting a little crazy." She took a sip of her drink. "But it was awful. My vision. I could see, hear and smell everything. So vividly." She shivered violently and Greg moved closer and put his arm around her.

"It's all fine now, you saved Reece and the other few hundred passengers today; you did an amazing thing."

"I couldn't have done it without your help." She looked at Violet. "Both of you."

Violet smiled. "I'm just so glad we were able to be there for you. It was a really scary situation."

"I just hope Reece gets in touch as soon as she gets there. I don't think I'll sleep properly until I know she has landed safely."

"It's amazing how you guys met, I can't believe how many Flames are reuniting at the moment." Violet smiled at Greg, and snuggled into his other side.

"How did you meet her? I missed that story earlier," Greg said.

"I was in the Gare du Nord, on my way to Spain…"

*   *   *

"Thank you for not sacking me," Aria said to Tim as they walked to work in the morning.

Tim chuckled. "I'm not that terrible a boss. You were in a bad way, I don't think sacking you would have helped in the slightest."

"No, it wouldn't have, but I would have understood. I mean, I was so moody and horrible to you."

"It was nothing I couldn't handle. Besides, even when you're moody, you're still a lot easier to deal with than my three sisters. They were a nightmare when they were in bad moods."

Aria smiled. "I don't know anything about your family.

You will have to tell me about them."

"I will. I will bore you with all the nitty gritty details one day."

They arrived outside the doors of the Butterfly Zoo, and Tim opened up. Aria followed him in, put her belongings in the staff room, and immediately started working, hoping to show Tim that although she may have been useless for the past few days, she was back on form now, and that she could be really useful and helpful. She tried not to think about the situation with Linen, and focused on her tasks instead. When she stepped into the butterfly enclosure, she felt lighter, and more relaxed.

Several hours later, she become aware that she was being watched. She looked up and caught Tim's eye. She smiled and he smiled back. He came over to her.

"How about that Faerie movie tonight?"

Aria nodded. "Okay, but can we have a drink first? I want to see if I can do the whole human thing, and talk to Linen."

"Sure, we'll stop by after work and see if he's there."

"Thank you."

Aria turned to speak to a visitor then, and Tim left to continue his rounds. She might have been imagining it, but she thought he looked a little disappointed when she'd mentioned talking to Linen. She shook the thought from her mind, and focused on her work.

By the end of the day, Aria was feeling really impatient to go and find Linen. She knocked on Tim's office door, and he called out for her to enter. "I'm done for the day," she announced as she stepped through the door.

He looked up and nodded. "I've just a couple more things to do, are you okay to wait for five minutes?"

Aria nodded and retreated from the room. She bounced around the staff room in anticipation, and finally, what felt like hours later, but was probably only about fifteen minutes, Tim emerged, his jacket on and keys in hand.

"Let's go," he said. Aria noticed the lack of enthusiasm in his voice, but she didn't mention it.

When they arrived at the pub, Tim went to the bar to get drinks for them both, and Aria headed straight for the piano. She was disappointed when she found the stool was empty.

"Are you looking for Theo?"

Aria looked up to see a pretty girl sitting at a nearby table, and frowned. "The piano guy?" she asked.

"Yes, Theo, the piano guy. He's out the back, getting ready, he'll be out in a minute."

"Oh, thank you. I'll wait here for him." A few minutes later, Theo emerged from the back room. He stopped short when he saw Aria standing there.

"Have you come to try and chop my fingers off again?" he asked, sarcasm dripping through his voice.

Aria shook her head quickly. "No, I wanted to apologise. I was really weird last time, and I'm sorry."

Theo raised an eyebrow. "More than a little weird. But, okay, apology accepted."

"It's just that you reminded me of someone, and you were playing a song like the one he wrote, and I guess I may have been a bit too intense in trying to explain it."

"A little intense, yes, I would agree with you there. Anyway, if you'll excuse me," he moved away from Aria, toward the girl sat at the table, he leaned down and they shared a long kiss. Aria watched, open-mouthed as the girl smiled up at him, then watched him walk over to the piano and sit down. Aria was too shocked to move as he started playing her song again, and finally, the girl shooed her away, looking annoyed with her.

Aria found Tim in a booth near the door. She sat down without a word and Tim sighed.

"Didn't go so well then?"

"He has a girlfriend," Aria said, her face white and her eyes starting to fill with tears. Tim pushed her drink toward her, and she picked it up and downed it in one gulp, wincing at the burn as the alcohol stung her throat. She set the empty glass back on the table. "I'm ready to go home now."

Tim looked down at his half-drunk pint and nodded. He gulped another mouthful down, then stood up and put his arm around Aria as they left. They didn't speak on the short walk home, and when they got in, instead of allowing Aria to go to her room and sink into despair again, Tim guided her to the living room, sat her on the sofa, put the movie on that he had bought for them to watch and put a large bowl of chocolate ice cream in her hands.

After a few minutes of tears streaming down her cheeks, Aria slowly started to eat the ice cream and lose herself in the movie. By the time it was half-way through, the ice cream was gone and she was even laughing at the funny parts. She looked over at Tim and caught him watching her. She smiled and mouthed, "Thank you."

"You're welcome."

*   *   *

"Guess what? I have a job!"

Ceri threw her arms around Charlie and hugged him. "Congratulations! That's great!"

Charlie kissed her. "Which means we can start saving up for our own place. After I've worked a couple of months, if we're really careful, we should have enough for a deposit and the first month."

"I have been saving as much of my wages as possible too, maybe we could do it even sooner than that."

"We'll start looking in a couple of weeks, would be good to see what's available."

"Sounds good. Now, what shall we do to celebrate?"

Charlie grinned. "My house is empty right now."

"Give me five minutes to grab my things, and I'll be right

with you." Ceri kissed Charlie quickly, then ran back into her house to pack her bag. She left the door slightly ajar, and a few minutes later, when it opened again, Charlie found himself face to face with her father.

"Hi, Mr Samson," Charlie said politely. "I'm just waiting for Ceri."

"Why did she leave you on the doorstep? Come on in, it's chilly today."

Charlie followed Ceri's father through the house, and into the kitchen. He stood awkwardly by the door while Mr Samson made himself a cup of tea. He offered Charlie one, but he declined.

"So what do you do, Charlie?"

Glad that he had just landed work, so that he could sounded like a more suitable suitor for Ceri, Charlie started telling him about his new job.

True to her word, Ceri was back before long, and she rescued Charlie from her father's interrogation. They left quickly, and Charlie carried her bag for her, as they walked toward his house.

"Your dad does know, right, that we're engaged?" Charlie asked casually. When he had said they should tell her parents together, she'd refused, saying she would tell them herself. He'd thought it a bit odd, but had let the subject drop because she had been agitated about it.

"I told my mum. I don't know if she mentioned it to Dad."

Charlie frowned. "Are you not very close? Surely getting married is a pretty big deal? Wouldn't your dad want to know?"

"No, we're not very close."

They walked in silence for a few minutes, Charlie could sense that there was something Ceri wasn't telling him, but he didn't want to completely kill the celebratory mood they'd been in earlier.

After they'd arrived at his house and settled in, Charlie

realised that Ceri hadn't said a word for a while, and he was starting to get worried. Not caring if it made the mood too sombre, when they got to his room, he sat her down on his bed, knelt down in front of her and took her hands.

"Ceri, please tell me what's going on with you right now. I'm worried."

Tears formed in Ceri's eyes, and with each one that fell, it was like a knife through Charlie's heart.

"I can't," she whispered.

"Why not? You can tell me anything, you know that. We're going to be married at some point, and we're moving in together, if there's something going on with you, I need to know what it is. Please."

"Promise me you won't go crazy? Because I don't need you to do anything about it."

Charlie frowned, but promised not to go crazy.

"My dad likes to drink, and when he's had too much..." Ceri looked up into Charlie's eyes. "You know I said those bruises were just from messing about with my brothers?" Charlie nodded, not liking where the conversation was going. "I lied. My dad was getting rough with my mum, so I intervened. He didn't like it, and taught me a lesson in interfering in other people's business."

Charlie tried to control his breathing, but his rage was simmering just under the surface. Though this time, it felt like a justified rage. He wanted to kill Mr Samson.

Ceri clocked the look in his eyes, and the change in his energy. She gripped his hands. "No, you promised you wouldn't go crazy. I don't need you to do anything stupid, just be with me. Just hold me and promise that we can be in our own place soon. That's all I need. Don't do anything stupid."

Charlie channelled all of his strength into calming his rage, trying to not storm out his house, march to Ceri's and beat her father to a pulp. Once he had calmed himself enough, he nodded. "Okay. I'm here. I'm calm." He leaned forward to kiss her, and she relaxed into his embrace.

"You make me feel safe. I don't worry about it all when I am with you."

Charlie pulled her closer to him, and they lay back on the bed. "You are safe. And there is no way you are going back to your house. You can live here with me until we get our own place."

"But-"

"No 'buts'. I won't take any excuses, you are not living there anymore. Okay?"

Ceri was quiet for a while. "I do worry about my mum and my brothers though. Although he doesn't seem to go for them so much. It's mostly just my mum, and me, when I get in the way."

Charlie held her tighter to him. "We will sort something out. I'll help you get all your stuff tomorrow."

"Okay."

*   *   *

"Do you know yet, why I am here?"

Gold looked at the Indigo Child, and allowed himself to ponder the question for a moment. His mind had been so full of Starlight, his heart had been so full of sorrow, that the presence of the Indigo Child, though welcome, had not had much of an impact on him. After a few moments, he was unable to grasp the reason, and shook his head. "No, I don't."

"I am here so that when you return home to the stars with your Flame, there will be someone to greet the souls and direct them on their way."

Gold raised his eyebrows. "How did you know about that?"

The Indigo Child tilted her head to one side. "I sensed it. As I have watched you during our time together, it is clear that you mean not to stay. And that you wish to be reunited with the one that holds your spark." She beckoned for Gold to come closer, and he knelt down in front of her. She put her hand to his heart.

"Your fire no longer burns as brightly, but you must keep fanning the flames until she returns. It is important."

Gold closed his eyes, and bowed his head. "I'm sorry I have not been fully present here with you, Indigo, but I have not been able to let go."

"But don't you see? You cannot let go. And you're not meant to. That is not the nature of Twin Flames. They are one with each other forever. No matter how much time and distance may appear to be separating them. Because of course, the separation is an illusion." The Indigo's voice dropped. "She is here," she whispered, tapping his heart lightly. "She is within you."

Gold opened his eyes and stared deeply into the bright blue eyes of the child. "She told me the exact same thing, not long ago. As did Pearl. And it is of course a concept that I know and understand and have taught. But it doesn't mean that it is how I feel."

The Indigo smiled, her whole face lighting up. "Don't you see how beautiful that is?"

Gold frowned. "Beautiful?"

"The strength of your love for her overrides everything. Logic, reason, knowledge, and wisdom are all meaningless when stood face to face with your love, your emotions and your connection to Starlight. Which is exactly how it should be."

Gold smiled, and stared into her eyes for a while. "My dear Indigo, your ability to see the truth that others are blind to is what makes you perfect for this role. Therefore I think you would do well. However, at the point where Starlight is likely to come back, and we will leave for the stars, will be the point when the rest of humanity will be in this dimension too, so there will be no one for you to greet from Earth. There won't be a civilisation there for millennia."

The Indigo Child smiled her knowing and wise smile. "We'll see."

*   *   *

"Leona! I have arrived in Sydney, but goodness, you wouldn't believe the drama at the airport."

Leona sighed with relief when she heard Reece's voice, and smiled at her words. "Really? What happened?" She let Reece launch into an explanation of the situation and the delay, but she didn't tell her about her own involvement in it all.

In the short time they had known each other, Leona had yet to mention her visions, preferring to wait for the right moment. She considered telling Reece when she was back in Paris, safe with her, but she didn't want to tell her when she still had another long plane journey ahead of her.

"My friends, Violet and Greg have come to visit me, and they're staying here, I hope that's okay."

Violet looked up at the mention of her name from her place on the sofa next to Greg. Leona smiled at her, then moved into the bedroom to continue her conversation.

"How is your mum?"

While Reece explained the situation, Leona ran her hand over a photograph of them both, which she had taken and printed out a couple of days before. She had framed it and placed the shell in front of it, the shell she had found on the beach when she'd had the vision of her Flame. She had also tucked a copy of the photo in a letter that she had hidden in Reece's luggage for her to find. She smiled at the thought of her finding it tucked away.

They didn't talk for long, aware that it would be costing a lot for the international call. After saying goodbye, Leona re-joined the others in the lounge.

Violet smiled up at her. "Is Reece okay?"

Leona nodded. "Yes, she's fine. And she has no idea that I had anything to do with the delay."

"You'll have to tell her about your visions at some point," Greg said. "It's not like you can hide them, you're on another planet when they're happening."

"I know, I'm just not quite ready yet. Besides, if you'd seen what I Saw," Leona shuddered. "You wouldn't want to tell the soul you loved more than anything in the world that you watched them die."

Greg's arm around Violet tightened, and a look crossed Violet's face that made Leona wonder about their reactions. She remembered her twenty-year vision, and wondered if they'd had similar visions. But instead of asking, she changed the subject. "So who's up for a croissant?"

Chapter Eight

After spending a couple of days with Leona in Paris, Greg and Violet said their goodbyes, and headed back to the countryside. They decided not to return to where they were HelpX-ing, but to go further south instead.

Though they had discussed their next move, the whole time they drove, moving further and further away from Paris, toward Spain, Violet felt uneasy, but couldn't explain why. She didn't mention it to Greg, though she knew he must be picking up on some of her uneasiness.

"Kind of puts everything into perspective, doesn't it?" Greg remarked a couple of hours into their journey.

"What does?"

"That anything could happen, at any moment. If it wasn't for Leona's vision, Reece would have been killed on that plane, and just a week after meeting her, Leona would have lost her Flame."

Violet nodded. "It does make you think. I mean, life is so transitional, so temporary. We really have no idea what is going to happen from moment to moment. All we can do is enjoy the moment we are experiencing."

"If that's true, then where have you been for the last couple of hours?"

Violet frowned. "I'm sorry. I just have this feeling of unease in my stomach. I know that travelling further south was what we planned, but something is telling me that we shouldn't be going so far away."

"So far away from what?"

"From the UK."

Without needing further explanation, Greg indicated and pulled off the road into the lay-by. He switched off the engine and turned his full attention to Violet. "Are we needed in the UK?"

Violet shrugged. "I don't know. I don't know what the feeling means."

"Then just let it be for a moment. Really feel into it. After the last couple of days, what I have really learned and realised is that we need to listen to these feelings, these intuitions, then act on them if we can. If I had ignored my feelings, I wouldn't have come to find you again. If I had let logic and reason come into it, I would have stayed with Leona. And if I had done that, she would never have met her Flame. And if she hadn't trusted her vision, her Flame would be dead right now."

Violet nodded. "I know what you are saying. I think it's important to listen too." She closed her eyes, and Greg did the same. She went within and asked herself what the feeling was. What it meant, what the answer was. But all she got was 'Help the Angels'.

She opened her eyes and told Greg. "The Earth Angels?" he asked.

She shook her head. "I don't know. That was all I got."

Greg leaned over to kiss her, straining against his seat belt. Then he started the engine again, and when the road was clear, he did a U-turn, and started driving back north. "We'll stop in the next place likely to have Wi-Fi and see if we can sort out a HelpX host to stay with. Or a campsite if we need to."

"Thank you. I'm sorry that our plans keep getting interrupted."

"Interruptions and obstacles are good. Without them, we would be on a never-ending, straight and boring path." Greg smiled over at Violet. "Besides, the bumps and changes seem easy to deal with when you are by my side, riding them out with me."

Violet smiled back. "I'm just glad we're here for each other. I know we can deal with anything together."

"Yes we can."

*   *   *

Despite not knowing who she really was, and being irritated by her crazy behaviour and her talk of other dimensions, Theo could not get the blonde-haired girl out of his head. Since she had tried to slam his fingers in the piano, he had dreamed of her every night. He would wake up next to his girlfriend, and wonder who she was, because she wasn't the one he loved.

The other thing that bothered him was that the song she claimed had been written for her by Linen, had just arrived in his mind one day. He remembered waking up and feeling really confused and disorientated, not sure who he was or where he was, but then his life had flooded back to him, with a few additions. Like the song. And a feeling that there was more to life than what his own currently contained.

Patty had started to notice that he wasn't as focused on her anymore, that his attention was elsewhere. And he hated that. They had been together for a long time, and she deserved better than that, so when he awoke for the fifth morning in a row with the face of the blonde girl in his mind, he decided to do something about it.

"Hey, Jay, you know the guy who comes in on Fridays, the tall skinny guy with short black hair? He came in here with the crazy blonde girl a few nights back?"

"The one that went psycho on you? Sure, I know the guy you mean."

"Do you know anything about him? Where he lives or works?"

The bartender raised an eyebrow. "You going to track down the psycho and press charges? I wouldn't blame you, but we could just bar her instead."

Theo shook his head. "No, nothing like that, I just want to talk to her."

"I think the guy owns the Butterfly Zoo, on the main road out of town. You might find him there. No idea about the girl though."

"Thanks, Jay. I appreciate it." Theo headed out of the pub. He needed to speak to the blonde girl, to Aria. He could have caught the bus to the zoo, but he preferred to walk. The air was frigid, but he barely noticed it as he strode along.

It took him fifteen minutes, but he finally approached the entrance to the zoo. He had never been there before, as butterflies had never interested him, but when he entered, he suddenly felt at home in the environment. He approached the ticket desk, where an older lady was sat behind the till.

"Hi there, I'm looking for the guy who owns the zoo?"

"Tim? He's in his office. May I ask why you would like to see him?"

"It's a personal matter," Theo said, for lack of a better reason.

The lady accepted this, and picked up her phone. She dialled a number and spoke to Tim, asking him to come to the front desk. "He'll be with you in a moment."

"Thanks."

She nodded at him, and he moved away from the desk to look at the posters on the walls of all the different types of butterflies. It was weird, but he could almost name them before seeing the accompanying text.

"Hi, can I help?"

Theo turned around to face Tim, and saw the recognition cross the man's face.

"Theo? You play the piano at the White Dragon Inn."

"Yes, I do. I was wondering if I could speak to you?"

Tim frowned but nodded and gestured for him to follow him to his office. Once seated and the door was closed, Tim spoke again. "So what can I help you with?"

"Aria."

Tim raised his eyebrows. "Do you remember her?"

"Of course, it's hard to forget an incident like that."

"No, I mean do you remember her from before?"

"Before what?" Theo was feeling a little irritated now, like Tim was privy to a secret that he was not.

"Before this life. Or, well, in your case, from before a couple of weeks ago, when you walked into this body."

Theo's eyebrows shot up. He began to wonder why he had come to see Tim; he was clearly just as nuts as the blonde. "Walked into this body? This is my body, what are you talking about?"

Tim frowned. "So why are you here?"

"I don't know. Because ever since the blonde went psycho on me, I have been dreaming about her, and it was driving me mad, so I came to talk to you and find out what the deal was. But clearly," Theo stood up and pushed the chair back. "You are all insane, so I'll just go."

"No, wait, we're not insane, I know it all sounds crazy, but it's not, I promise. You know Aria, you were together in your previous existence. You worked together on the Other Side, at the Earth Angel Training Academy. You are both Faeries, or, well, you were."

Theo blinked several times, then held his hand up. "Right, okay, yeah. Thanks." He left the office quickly, before Tim could stop him. He exited the zoo, and didn't slow his pace until he was a good distance away.

"Faeries?" he muttered to himself as he walked. "Did he honestly expect me to believe that I used to be a Faerie? Mental."

When he arrived home, Patty came running out of the bedroom and jumped on him. "Where have you been?"

He caught her and they kissed. "Just had to go to the pub for something. Sorry, babe, did you miss me?"

"Yes, I did! Now come back to bed."

Theo laughed. "It's two in the afternoon."

"So?" Theo allowed Patty to lead him to the bedroom, and did his best to clear all thoughts of blonde Faeries from his mind.

*   *   *

"Charlie! Stop!"

Through the red haze clouding his vision, Charlie looked up to see his Flame, his beautiful beloved, with tears streaming down her cheeks and her hands covering her mouth.

He blinked and the red haze began to clear. He looked down and the first thing he registered was the blood covering his hands, the second thing was the lifeless body of Mr Samson pinned underneath the weight of his own.

"What have you done?" Ceri cried. She stepped toward them, and Charlie shook his head to try and clear it.

"I don't know what happened, I just… I just saw him and I snapped." He struggled to stand and move away. His hands hung limply at his sides, the fight had left him completely.

Ceri's mother arrived in the kitchen then, and when she registered the scene in front of her, she started screaming. Ceri tried to calm her, but in the end had to take her out of the room. "Call an ambulance!" she said over her shoulder to Charlie. But he couldn't move. Several minutes later, Ceri returned, phone in hand.

"Ambulance, please," she whispered into the phone. She knelt at her father's side and slowly reached out to touch his neck, searching for a pulse. When her head bowed, Charlie's heart thudded.

Had he just killed a man? Not just any man, but the father of his Twin Flame?

Ceri gave her address to the emergency services, and Charlie remained rooted to the spot. When she explained the situation, he knew then, that there would be no way out of this. He had just killed another human being, and he was going to pay the price for it.

When Ceri hung up, she stayed at her father's side for a minute, staring down at his bloody and broken body. Then she looked up at Charlie, and the pain and heartbreak in her eyes tore him in two. But worse than that, he saw something else, something he never imagined he would see in her eyes.

Fear.

She was afraid of him. She had seen what he was capable of now. She had seen what his rage truly looked like. And she wouldn't ever trust him again. He could see that.

The next hour passed in a blur. The police arrived with the ambulance, breaking up their tableau of pain and horror. He was cuffed and arrested, and as he was taken away, he saw the paramedics work futilely on Mr Samson, while Ceri stood there watching.

She looked up at him. "I'm sorry," he mouthed.

Tears streamed down her cheeks, but she didn't respond.

He was bundled into the back of a police car, and as they drove away, all he was aware of was the stickiness of the blood drying on his hands, and the lone tear that was making its way down his cheek.

*   *   *

"You look beautiful."

Starlight smiled up at Gareth. "Thank you. You're looking quite handsome yourself." She smiled when he blushed at the compliment, and happily took the hand he offered to help her out of the taxi. He closed the car door, then turned to her, still holding her hand.

"I hope this place is okay for you," he said, nodding

toward the restaurant. "It's got great reviews."

"I'm sure it'll be fantastic," Starlight said, as they walked toward the entrance.

Once seated inside, Starlight ignored the menu and instead stared at the man in front of her. He was as different to Gold as it was possible to be, and yet there was something that drew her to him.

He looked up from the menu and smiled back. He set it down and returned her gaze. "Did you get your results back yet?"

She nodded. "Yes. They couldn't find anything wrong with me at all. How about you?"

"Same. Let me ask you something," he leaned closer. "Have you had any headaches since we met?"

Starlight thought for a moment, then shook her head. "No, I haven't. Have you?"

"No. Not one." He shook his head and sat back in his seat. "It makes you wonder, doesn't it?"

"You think we got those headaches just so that we would be brought together?" It was an interesting idea, and not something that Starlight had considered up to that point.

"Or that we healed each other somehow."

"Are you a healer?" Starlight asked, suddenly aware that she knew very little of the man who sat before her. Other than some of his medical history.

"Not that I am aware of. But then, there are many things I am sure I'm not aware of."

Starlight smiled. How right he was. She picked up her menu. "I think regardless of how it all happened, we need to celebrate the fact that we no longer have headaches."

"How about we celebrate the fact that we have met instead?"

"Sounds like a plan."

They were quiet for a few minutes while they read the menus, then the waiter appeared and filled their glasses with wine and took their order. The conversation flowed easily, and for a few hours, Starlight forgot that she was the Angel of Destiny, on Earth for a very important mission, and enjoyed feeling like a normal human being, on a wonderful first date with a lovely man.

Gareth walked her home, and when they reached the entrance to the apartment block, they lingered at the door for a while, unable to say goodnight.

"I have work in the morning, I should go," Gareth murmured.

Starlight nodded. "Yes, I wouldn't want you to be too tired and oversleep."

Gareth shifted from one foot to the other, and Starlight smiled inwardly at his nervousness. She knew that he wanted to kiss her, and she wanted to kiss him too, but she knew that it was customary to allow the man to make that first move. "Okay, thank you for a lovely evening," he said.

"Thank you for dinner, it really was amazing" Starlight replied. She reached into her bag, pulled her keys out, and decided to ignore normal human etiquette. She leaned forward and softly touched her lips to his. His sharp intake of breath signalled to her that he was caught off guard, but he recovered in seconds and he deepened the kiss.

When they finally pulled apart, Starlight smiled at him. "Goodnight, Gareth." She unlocked the door and went inside. When she looked back through the glass of the door, she saw him still standing there, a smile on his face.

He waved, then walked away, down the road toward his home.

Starlight went up the stairs, ignoring the lift. When she reached the apartment and let herself in, she was surprised to see Hannah still sat in the lounge, watching TV.

"Hey," she said.

Hannah looked up. "Hey yourself. Did you have a good evening?"

Starlight nodded and slipped her coat and shoes off. She went over and settled on the sofa next to Hannah, who offered her half of the blanket that was covering her. Starlight accepted it gratefully, and relaxed back into the cushions.

"It was a lovely date. Not that I have anything to compare it to, but I think it went really well."

"Did you kiss him?" Hannah asked, switching the TV off.

Starlight laughed. "Yes, I did. He was so nervous, that I didn't think he was going to make a move, so I did instead. I know it's not the done thing, but I wanted to see what it would be like."

"And what was it like?"

Starlight frowned. "Have you had a boyfriend, Hannah?"

Hannah sighed. "I haven't really met anyone I want to be with." She shrugged. "I don't think the Twin Flame concept applies to Indigos. After all, we cannot have Indigo Flames, because we are all brothers and sisters, there is no romantic love between us. And we are unlikely to have Flames who are human or from other realms."

Starlight considered this for a moment. She allowed herself to go deep within and access the wisdom of the stars that she held. "Your capacity to love unconditionally means you do not need to have a Twin Flame connection to experience that kind of love. But it is possible for the Indigos to have Flames. They may be Crystals, Earth Angels or humans."

Hannah smiled. "I love how you can just connect like that. You must teach me how. I feel as though I am losing my connection to my siblings." She sighed. "I remember that the early Indigos lost their connection to us, to their home, and they became adrift from their purpose."

Starlight reached out to touch Hannah's arm. "That will not happen to you, sweet Indigo. I can tell you that with absolute faith."

"Thank you." Hannah yawned. "I think I should go to bed,

I have to work tomorrow."

"I think I need to find some form of employment," Starlight remarked. "I cannot live on your hospitality forever."

Hannah smiled. "You know it is no burden to me." She shook her head. "It just seems so weird, that the Angel of Destiny should have to get an ordinary job to earn money to live on." She chuckled. "It's a weird collision between the eternal ethereal realm and the illusionary physical realm we find ourselves in."

"It is," Starlight agreed. "I didn't really know what to expect, coming here. Being human. It is quite odd."

Hannah stood up and stretched. "But in a good way, right?"

Starlight remembered the look of shock on Gareth's face as she kissed him. "Yes, in a good way."

*   *   *

Reece watched her mother's pale, sleeping face and sighed. Her mother's condition had been deteriorating rapidly over the last few hours, and Reece didn't want to leave her bedside. She had called other members of the family, and they had come to visit throughout the day. She didn't think it would be long before her mother made her transition to the Other Side.

She stroked her veiny, bony hand, and wished she had more time with her. More chances to apologise for their rift, more moments to hug her, to laugh with her, to tell her she loved her.

"Mum," she whispered. "There's something you need to know. I met the one I love. The one I want to spend the rest of my life with. Her name is Leona, and we met in Paris." There was no change in her mother's state, but she continued anyway, feeling relief at finally telling her mother about her true self.

"I love her. She's so beautiful. And when our bodies

entwine, our souls become one and there is nowhere else on this planet I would rather be than with her." She bit her lip. "It actually hurts to be so far away from her, now that I know her smell, her touch, her presence. Can you understand that? Did you have that with Dad?"

Though she didn't expect a response, Reece paused and waited, as if it were possible. When there was still no change, she continued.

"I know that our connection goes beyond this world, and goes back further than we can imagine. It's eternal. As we are all eternal." Reece wasn't even sure where the words were coming from now, but she felt it was important to say. Her voice became a little louder, and she didn't care if anyone else in the hospital ward heard her. She wanted to make her sure her mum heard her words.

"We are eternal. We are one. I love you so much." Tears sprang to her eyes, and she slipped her hand around her mother's. "I know that you loved me unconditionally, and I think that is how I can love Leona fully now. How I can give her all of me. It's okay, to let go now, because death is simply another part of life. You will still exist, you will still be with me."

She noticed that her mother's breathing was becoming slower, and shallower.

"I love you, Mum, you can let go now. It's okay. You will be greeted by the Angels, you can go home."

As she uttered the word 'home' her mother let out a small gasp, then fell silent. Reece watched her chest for a few moments, and it no longer rose and fell with breath, but was completely still. She closed her eyes and allowed her tears to fall.

"She's gone?"

Reece felt a hand on her shoulder and looked up to see her sister stood beside her. She nodded, and her sister's face crumpled. She let go of her mother's hand and stood up to embrace her sister, holding her until her sobs subsided.

"She's gone home now. The Angels will take care of her now. She's safe."

Chapter Nine

"I feel a bit silly."

Greg stopped digging for a minute, and looked up at Violet, who was kneeling in the soil, pulling out weeds. "Why do you feel silly?"

"Because I made us change our plans, and stay closer to the UK, and for what? It's been five weeks now, and we keep hovering around the north, waiting for some reason why we are needed here." Violet shook the dirt from the roots of some weeds and threw them into the basket beside her. "But nothing has happened. I think maybe I was wrong."

Greg shrugged. "Does it matter? We've met some great people, found hosts to stay with, and we are still doing what we wanted, just in a different location. I don't feel like I am waiting for something to happen. Do you?"

"Yes." Violet sat back on her heels. "I feel like something is brewing. But it's silly, because when the drama with Leona happened, there was no warning at all, it all happened completely out of the blue. So to feel on edge like this is doing me in."

Greg set his fork down, and went over to Violet, holding out a hand to help her up. When they were face to face, he looked deeply into her eyes. "This moment is the only thing that matters right now. And in this moment we are together, and in love. Stop waiting for something bad to happen. If something bad happens, we will deal with it in that moment, okay?"

Violet smiled. "Okay." She leaned in to kiss Greg, and he wrapped his arms around her waist, drawing her in closer. "How about we have a quick break," she suggested.

Greg chuckled. "I think you read my mind."

They left their weeding and headed back to their van, stopping by the outside tap to wash their hands on the way. They climbed into the van and pulled the door closed behind them. Despite the chill in the air of the early spring, they quickly stripped down out of their work clothes and got under the covers.

"Do you think we'll ever tire of one another?" Violet asked, as she traced her finger down his bare chest.

"I hope not," Greg responded. "I hope that we are as madly in love with each other when we are old and wrinkled, as we are now."

"Hey, less of the old and wrinkly talk, please. I plan to grow old very gracefully."

A flash of Violet with lines creasing her face and flowing grey hair flashed through Greg's mind and he nodded. "You will look beautiful at every stage of your life," he said. "I have no doubt about that."

Violet grinned. "You do know how to make a girl feel special." She leaned in to kiss him and then jumped when she heard a noise coming from the side drawer. It took her a moment to register that it was her mobile phone ring-tone. She frowned and her heartbeat quickened, could Leona be in trouble again?

She reached over and pulled the drawer open, and dug around to find the phone. She glanced at the display before answering, and her heart plummeted into her stomach.

"Hello?"

"Violet?"

Violet frowned when she heard the voice filtering through.

"Mike? Is that you?" Greg sat upright when he heard the tone of her voice.

"Yes," Mike replied, his voice breaking. "Violet, it's Esmeralda. She's…"

Violet's heart thudded when his voice dissolved into sobs. "Shh, it's okay, Mike, tell me what's happening."

"She's dying, Violet. And I don't know how long she has left. Please come."

Tears sprang to Violet's eyes, and she swallowed hard. "Oh, Mike," she whispered. "We will be there as soon as we possibly can. Tell her we will be there soon." Greg wrapped his arm around her as she began to shake.

All she heard in reply was Mike's heart-wrenching sobs, then the line went dead. She pulled the phone away from her ear, then stared at it until the screen went black.

"What is it? What's happened?" Greg asked.

"It's Esmeralda," Violet replied, her voice shaking. "Mike said she's dying."

"What? Are you serious?"

Violet nodded, then started to sob. Greg wrapped her in his embrace, and held her tight.

When she calmed down a little, she pulled away and got out of the bed. She started to pull on her clothes, and Greg followed suit. With an overwhelming sense of déjà vu, this time it was Greg that went to explain to their hosts that they needed to leave, and within half an hour, they were on the road, heading back to England.

Greg wanted to comfort Violet, but his own heart was in pieces. Memories of a life he had never lived were flashing through his mind. Hearing of Violet's death, standing in front of her grave, collapsing onto the fresh grass, and sobbing for the woman he had loved so deeply, yet lost because of his own inability to allow that love in.

He was glad they would be there for Mike, but he knew that they wouldn't be able to offer him the comfort he needed.

Because after losing a Twin Flame, he knew that it felt as though nothing would ever make you smile again.

*   *   *

"Tim, what's happening?"

Tim looked down at the beautiful woman in his arms and shook his head. "I don't know," he whispered. "But I really want to kiss you right now."

Aria's eyes were wide, but she didn't pull away. After finding out that Linen, or Theo, rather, had come to look for her, but then had rejected the notion of their previous life together, Aria had been in despair. She was so thankful that Tim had been there for her every day, making her smile, comforting her, being her best friend. But in the last week, it had been more than just friendship sparking between them. Every time they came into contact, she felt like the butterflies weren't just flying around her, but in her stomach too.

Tim leaned down and kissed her softly on the lips, and she closed her eyes, surrendering to his embrace. It wasn't as electrically charged as when she and Linen used to kiss, in the Fifth Dimension, but there was something about Tim's touch that made her feel safe and loved, and that was what she needed in that moment. She returned the kiss, and reached up to run her hand through his short hair. He sighed into her mouth and deepened his kisses.

After a few minutes, Aria pulled back. "I feel a bit strange."

Tim released her and bowed his head. "I'm sorry. I didn't mean to overstep the mark, I know your heart belongs to Linen,"

Aria reached up to put her finger to Tim's lips. "Shh. You didn't overstep the mark, I just feel a bit weird that's all. And if things go wrong, I don't want to lose your friendship, you're the only friend I have here on Earth."

Tim shook his head. "No matter what happens, I promise you will never lose me as a friend. Ever."

Aria smiled. "Good." She tilted her head up and he took that as an invitation to kiss her again. He happily obliged, and once more they melted into one another.

When they finally came up for air, Tim suggested they go for a walk. He knew that Aria loved being outside, and besides, if they stayed indoors much longer, he wasn't going to be able to stop himself from taking things further with her, and he was determined to take things slowly.

They headed for the local park, and despite the slight chill in the air, the spring sunshine was warm. Tim was glad they had taken the day off; sometimes he forgot that there was more to life than just working, but Aria was doing a great job of reminding him of that.

"Hey, this is where we first met!" Aria let go of his hand and skipped toward the lawn where he had first seen her dancing. She danced on the grass, twirling joyfully and unashamedly, making Tim smile.

"I couldn't believe how beautiful you were, lost in your own world, dancing barefoot and carefree," Tim remarked.

Aria stopped dancing and opened her eyes to look at him. "You thought I was beautiful? I was even more beautiful with wings."

"I think you're beautiful in every form."

Aria blushed and ran back toward him. She came to stop just inches away. "Do you love me?"

Tim blinked at the question, so sudden and direct. But he already knew the answer. "Yes. I do love you, Aria."

Aria's face broke into a grin and she leaned forward to kiss him. She then stepped back and smiled. "I love you too, alien."

Tim laughed and she danced away again, looking very much like the Faerie she really was.

*   *   *

"And how do you find the defendant?"

"Guilty, your honour."

Charlie dropped his head, and his heart thudded painfully in his chest. It was all over. He looked over his shoulder to where Ceri sat with her mother, and his heart screamed in pain at the sight of the tears streaming down her cheeks. He couldn't even bring himself to look at Mrs Samson. It all seemed like such a nightmare. He went to sleep in his cell every night, praying, wishing, and hoping that he would wake up in his own bed, with Ceri pressed up close to him, her beautiful form entwined with his. But it didn't happen.

He wrenched his gaze from Ceri's and looked over to where his mother sat. She was sobbing too, and he mouthed "I'm so sorry" to her. She nodded slightly in acknowledgement, but he knew that nothing he did or said would ever change things now.

They were all dismissed by the judge, his sentence was to be decided in the following week, but he had been found guilty of murder. At best he was looking at fifteen years. At worst, it would be life in prison. In that moment, Charlie was incapable of moving. He had to be almost lifted to his feet by the guard, and dragged back to the van that would take him back to prison.

Just as they were about to pass through the door, he heard someone call out for them to stop. He looked up to see Ceri approaching. Her red, tear-stained face was set in what Charlie feared was a permanent frown.

She got within touching distance, but didn't close the gap, for fear it wouldn't be allowed. "May I give him a hug?" she asked the guard. He nodded quickly, and Ceri reached out and wrapped her frail arms around Charlie's frame. He had lost a lot of weight in the past few weeks, but his frame still eclipsed her own.

"I love you," she whispered into his ear. With those words, he began to sob. She held his shaking body for a few more seconds before the guard cleared his throat and asked her to step away.

She did so reluctantly, letting go and stepping back.

"I love you too," Charlie choked out. "I'm so sorry."

Ceri nodded and Charlie allowed the guards to take him away. He had no idea when he would next get to hold his Flame, if ever again.

*   *   *

"Starlight, are you okay?"

Starlight sat next to the toilet, feeling miserable. She shook her head at Hannah, who was peering round the bathroom door. Hannah came in, and crouched down next to her. "Have you eaten something bad?"

Starlight shook her head. "I don't think so, I just feel really sick."

Hannah reached out to touch her forehead, but Starlight didn't have a fever. She frowned. "How long have you been feeling sick?"

Starlight thought for a moment. "Just the last few days. It's only when I wake up though, I'm fine later on."

"Ah," Hannah said, her eyes widening.

"Ah?" Starlight repeated, wiping her mouth with the back of her hand.

"Have you thought about doing a pregnancy test?" From the look of shock on Starlight's face, Hannah guessed that she hadn't thought of that. "Tell you what, get yourself cleaned up, and I'll pop out to the shops and get one."

She got up and headed to the door, but when she looked back to see that Starlight hadn't moved, she returned to her and helped her to her feet. "It's okay," she said, smiling. "It might not be that, but it would be good to know whether it is or not."

"Pregnant?" Starlight whispered. "But I've only known

- 123 -

Gareth for a few weeks, what will he say?"

"I'm sure he will be over the moon, that man is besotted with you. Now get cleaned up and dressed, I'll be back soon." Hannah left and Starlight heard the clinking of keys and the front door of the apartment open and slam closed.

She went over to the mirror and stared at her pale reflection. There was something different about her. She could see it. She rested a hand on her stomach and marvelled at the idea that there could be a tiny being growing there. She sighed and thought of Gold. Though she loved Gareth, and was acclimatising to being on Earth, she missed her Flame so much sometimes, it was like a physical ache in her heart, in the core of her soul.

Starlight was still hanging onto the sink, and staring into the mirror when Hannah returned. She came back into the bathroom, and saw that Starlight hadn't moved. She set the bag down, and patiently helped Starlight clean her hands and face, and then guided her out to the lounge. She made a cup of tea and some toast, and set it in front of the Angel.

Starlight ate and drank gratefully, and started to come to life a little. "Thank you," she said. "I don't know why I am falling apart like this."

Hannah smiled. "If you are pregnant, then it will be the hormones wreaking havoc, but let's wait to see."

Starlight nodded, and when she had gathered enough courage, she returned to the bathroom to do the test.

When she emerged a few minutes later, holding the stick complete with two lines, Hannah was still sat at the table waiting. "You were right."

Hannah smiled and got up to hug the Angel. "Congratulations, you will be an amazing mother."

Starlight was in shock. "I guess I should get myself sorted and go see Gareth." She shook his head. "What if this isn't what he wants?"

"He wants you, he will be happy. Trust me."

"Thank you." She headed back to the bathroom to shower, wondering how she was going to tell Gareth the news. While she stood under the hot water, she silently prayed that Gold would be happy for them both. She knew that his heart had been broken when she left him, she'd hate to think he was still in pain.

Over an hour later, she knew she couldn't stall any longer. She had called Gareth and arranged to meet in their favourite coffee shop. At least if they were somewhere public, he couldn't get too upset. She really had no idea if he would be happy about the news or not, despite Hannah's reassurances.

Half an hour later, she was sat in the coffee shop, nervously playing with the empty sugar packets. Gareth came in and spotted her. He grinned and came over to her, and she got up to greet him. They kissed slowly for several seconds, and Starlight knew in that moment that everything was going to work out.

Once they were settled and Gareth had his order in front of him, Starlight decided to just say it quickly.

"Gareth, I'm pregnant."

*   *   *

Leona paced up and down the tiny lounge, feeling too nervous to sit still. Reece was due to arrive back in Paris, after having been away in Australia for five weeks. She had stayed on to arrange her mother's funeral and settle all her affairs, before finally feeling she could leave and come back to Europe. To Leona.

After everything that she had been through, Leona hoped that Reece didn't feel differently about their relationship. That she wouldn't see her again and decide that she didn't want to be with her. She was also so worried about her being on a plane. She hadn't slept in the last twenty-four hours, watching the TV intently to see if there were any news items. She hadn't had any further visions since the plane crash and news report, but it didn't mean that something terrible wouldn't happen.

Finally, the clock said that it was an acceptable time to go to the airport to meet her Flame. She walked to the metro, picking up a bunch of roses from a street seller on the way.

When she got there, she hopped from foot to foot, and tried not to look suspicious; the memory of being pinned down by security was still fresh in her mind, even after several weeks. When the passengers from the Australian flight started to come through, Leona stopped hopping and strained to see her beloved through the crowd.

When she finally spotted her, her heart started pounding and she made her way to her side. When Reece saw her, she dropped all her luggage and threw her arms around her, kissing her deeply. Leona returned the kiss, not caring that they were in the middle of a busy airport. Eventually, Leona drew back and smiled. She looked at Reece's face carefully and saw the tiredness and the sadness in her eyes, but also an overwhelming passion.

"I am so glad to be back," Reece said. "I missed you so much."

Leona held out the now slightly squashed bunch of roses to her Flame. "You have no idea how glad I am to see you. It feels like it's been a lifetime since you left."

Reece took the flowers and breathed in their scent. "Two lifetimes," she said with a smile. She reached down to pick up her discarded handbag, and Leona took the handle of her suitcase. They headed for the exit, and Leona wrapped her free arm around Reece. The whole way back to the apartment, they didn't stop talking.

Reece told her all about her mother's transition to the Other Side, and the funeral, and how the whole family had become so much closer as a result of it all. She had also talked with her family about how she had felt rejected by them because of her preferences.

"You said that to them? Really?" Leona asked, as they entered the apartment.

"Yes, I did. I told them all about you, and how I felt about you. And after they got used to the idea, they were completely okay with it."

Leona set down the case then threw her arms around Reece and kissed her. "That's brilliant. I'm so glad they were cool with it."

Reece nodded. "Me too. The only thing they weren't cool about was me leaving you behind and not taking you there with me to meet them."

"See? Didn't I tell you it would be fine?"

"You did."

Leona went to make them both drinks, and Reece removed her outer clothing before flopping onto the settee and closing her eyes. Before Leona could bring a drink back to her, she was already fast asleep, and snoring softly. Leona smiled at her exhausted Flame and put the drinks down on the table. She grabbed a blanket from the armchair and placed it over Reece, tucking it in so she wouldn't get cold. She kissed her softly on the forehead, then sat next to her on the settee, and picked up the book she had been reading earlier but couldn't concentrate on. Now that Reece was by her side again, she felt like she could relax. She knew it would be fine from then on.

Chapter Ten

It seemed to take an age, but finally, Violet and Greg were driving down the familiar potholed lane to the Twin Flame Retreat. They pulled into the parking area, and then jumped out of the van, into the twilit clearing. Violet looked up at the full moon through the trees and sighed. It was so beautiful. She was just sad that they were there for such a horrible reason. Hand in hand, they made their way toward the house.

"Oh, Angel," Violet said, letting go of Greg's hand and walking quickly up to the steps of the house where Mike stood, looking as though he had aged ten years in the last couple of months. They hugged for a long time.

"How is she, Mike?" Greg asked.

Violet pulled back from Mike and he shook his head. "Not good. She sleeps most of the time now. Come up to see her, I told her you were coming."

"It's so fast, what happened?"

Mike ushered them in and once inside, he closed the front door and spoke in a hushed voice. "About three weeks ago, Esmeralda finally went to the doctors to get a lump checked, that she found four months ago. Within a week, they tested it, and there was nothing they could do, it had already spread everywhere. She went downhill so fast after that."

Violet could feel the tears streaming down her cheeks. She hugged Mike again, then they made their way through the front room, which no longer looked like the clean and cosy Twin Flame Retreat she remembered, but instead looked like an unkempt bachelor pad. Violet looked around and decided that even if she could do nothing else to help, she would sort the house out; Esmeralda always kept it so beautiful, she wouldn't want it to be like this.

Violet gripped Greg's hand tightly as they went upstairs and entered the bedroom, and as she stood with Greg and Mike around the bed, her vision from the last time she had been there came back to her. She had known it would be for a sad occasion, but she could never have imagined this. She approached the bed, and her heart shuddered at the sight of Esmeralda looking so pale and thin, her eyes closed and her chest rising and falling with shallow breaths.

"Esmeralda?" she said softly, approaching the bedside. The Incarnated Angel's eyes fluttered at the sound of her name, and after a few seconds, they opened. Her lips curved into a slight smile.

"Violet. You came." Her whispered words, uttered so breathlessly, brought more tears to Violet's eyes.

"Oh, Angel," Violet whispered. She reached out to take Esmeralda's hand, and squeezed it gently. "You should have called for us sooner."

"It all happened so fast," Esmeralda said. "We had no idea it would be so soon."

Violet looked up at Mike, who seemed like he was about to collapse. "When was the last time you ate, Mike?" Violet asked.

Greg took his cue, and put his arm around Mike's shoulder. "Let's go get something to eat," he said, guiding his friend to the door. Greg looked back to Violet and she nodded.

"You are so beautiful, Angel," she said to Esmeralda. "If it weren't for you, Greg and I would never have come back together. How will the world go on without you?"

"It was my most important mission, to make sure the two

of you were together again." The long sentence seemed to tire her, and she closed her eyes. "Violet, please promise me something," she breathed, her eyes opening again.

"Anything," Violet replied, tears now streaming down her face.

"Make sure Mike is okay. I don't think he's coping very well with all of this." A tear trickled down Esmeralda's cheek. "Twin Flames are not meant to be apart," she said, her voice getting a little stronger in her conviction.

Violet nodded in agreement. "You are right, dear Angel. They are not."

"But it seems it is time for me to go home." Esmeralda closed her eyes again, and her breathing slowed down, making Violet's heart thud painfully. "The Angels are calling me."

Violet gripped her friend's hand. Afraid that Esmeralda was about to slip away, and that Mike was going to miss saying goodbye, she got up and went to the top of the stairs. "Mike! Greg!" she called. She heard a thundering of footsteps come through the living room and up the stairs, as she returned to the bedroom. Mike came in, and went straight to Esmeralda. He took his Twin Flame's hand.

"My love?" he whispered.

Violet was grateful for Greg's strong arms encircling her, as they watched Esmeralda open her eyes.

"I know we will be together again," she whispered. "Do not fear, I will watch over you always."

"I will not rest until I find you and am with you again," Mike replied.

Esmeralda smiled and closed her eyes for the last time. Mike kissed her on the forehead, and on the lips. Her body shuddered once then became still. When he realised that his Flame had left him, Mike let out a wail that would haunt Violet for the rest of her life.

*   *   *

Aria couldn't quite believe how things had turned out. She had left the Other Side, hand in hand with her Twin Flame, only to get to Earth and end up falling in love with her alien room-mate? It was a little bizarre. She watched Tim sleeping for a while, feeling both happy and sad at the same time. She was happy that she had found Tim, and that he had rescued her, taken her in, cared for her and now loved her. But she was sad that she would never feel as deeply for him as she did for Linen.

She sighed and closed her eyes. It did feel nice to be wrapped up next to him though. Despite it being nearly spring, it was still so cold. She remembered the winters when she was in the Elemental Realm, but somehow, they didn't seem as bitterly cold as the one they'd just had. Perhaps it was because the Elemental Realm was vibrating at a higher rate.

Unable to fall asleep again with all the thoughts whirring around her head, Aria slid out of bed and grabbed Tim's dressing gown to wrap herself in. She quietly left the room and headed for the kitchen, thinking it would be nice if she could make breakfast for Tim, and surprise him.

Despite watching him over the past few weeks in the kitchen, her cooking skills were still severely lacking, after all, she was used to just manifesting her snacks out of thin air on the Other Side. Actually putting ingredients together and creating an edible outcome was a little beyond her still. In the end, she settled for boiled eggs, slightly burnt toast, and some fresh fruit. She made coffee, and then piled it all onto a tray and took it into Tim's bedroom, where he was beginning to stir.

"Wakey wakey sleepyhead," Aria sang, trying to navigate her way over the discarded clothing on the floor without tripping up. Tim opened his eyes and blinked at her. His mouth curved into a smile at the sight of her, and he pulled himself into a sitting position, while yawning and stretching.

"Breakfast in bed? I think this may be the first ever time for me."

Aria smiled and set the tray down in front of him, before she climbed back into bed. "Last night was my first time ever as a human, so it's a time of firsts all round."

Tim's eyes widened. "Wow, I hadn't even thought about that." He shook his head. "I didn't want to go so fast, I wanted to take things slowly, but then I don't know, I didn't want to stop, I'm so sorry."

Aria giggled. "Don't apologise. I didn't want to stop either." She leaned in to kiss him. "I had a lovely night, and I'm not sorry that we are moving fast. Faeries are impatient creatures, didn't you know?" She nabbed a boiled egg, and took the top off before dipping a strip of toast in it.

"So I gather," Tim said with a smile. He followed suit and tucked into the other boiled egg. "Is this the first time you've boiled an egg too?"

Aria frowned. "Yes, why? What's wrong with it?"

"Nothing, it's perfect," Tim said, dipping his toast in the yolk. "I'm just impressed at how well you do things for the first time."

Aria beamed with pleasure at the praise. "That's just because we Faeries are awesome. Get used to it."

Tim laughed, nearly choking on his mouthful. He swallowed quickly then leaned over to kiss her. "I plan to."

*   *   *

"Mum?"

Ceri's mother looked up at her from her place on the sofa, where she was staring into space and biting her thumbnail. "What?" she asked.

Ceri went over and sat next to her. "Are you okay?"

Her mother sighed, her red eyes blinking tiredly. "I don't know." She looked over to the door, which was slightly open, then lowered her voice so that Ceri's brothers wouldn't overhear her. "I feel so guilty," she said, pain etched in her features.

"Guilty? What for?"

"For feeling happy that he is gone."

Ceri's eyes widened. She hadn't been expecting her mother to say that.

"I know, I know, it's an awful thing to say, a terrible thing to feel, but-"

"It's not terrible or awful at all," Ceri cut in, putting her hand on her mother's. "I feel the same way. Simultaneously happy and guilty and sad. I just wish it hadn't happened that way."

"Me too."

They sat in silence for a few moments, then Ceri took a deep breath. "I still want to marry Charlie."

It was her mother's turn to be shocked.

"I know what he did was terrible, but he only did it because he loved me so much," Ceri's voice cracked. "He's my Twin Flame, Mum, and I don't expect you to understand that, but I know that I will never love anyone as much as I love him, and I don't want to give up on him, because of what he did. I love him too much."

Ceri's mother was quiet for a while, then slowly she nodded. "Part of me doesn't understand, but that's because I have never felt love of that depth, other than for you and your brothers. But there is a part of me, deep in my heart, that gets it. You have my blessing, if that was what you were looking for."

Tears started streaming down Ceri's cheeks. "Your blessing was more than I could have hoped for."

Ceri's mother smiled, then reached out to hug her. They hugged for a long time, united in their grief and hope. When they pulled apart, Ceri's mother frowned. "How does it even work? Marrying someone in prison?"

Ceri shook her head. "I have no idea, but I'm going to find out. I'm going to court for the sentencing, and I will tell him then, that no matter how long the sentence, I will wait for him."

"I admire your courage, your strength, and your ability to love so deeply," her mother said. "It gives me hope that you haven't been too damaged by the abuse you suffered here." Her face crumpled and she began to sob. "I'm so sorry I wasn't strong enough to get us away from him."

They hugged again, and Ceri held her mother until the sobbing subsided. "You have nothing to apologise for. You loved us all unconditionally, and we got through it because of that."

Just then, the door opened, and without needing any explanation, Ceri's brothers all came in and joined in with the hug. She decided that she would ensure her family was okay, and that their health and happiness would be her mission until her Flame returned home to her.

*   *   *

"Emerald! My dear, sweet Angel, you are home." Gold held out his arms to welcome her, and she stepped into them, hugging the Old Soul hard.

"Oh, Gold, how are you?" Emerald pulled away and looked down to address the small Indigo Child at his side. "Indigo! What are you doing here?"

"She simply wanted to see this side of things," Gold said, not allowing the Child to explain. The Indigo frowned a little at him, but didn't contradict him. Emerald knelt down to hug her too.

She stood back up and smiled at Gold. "Velvet and Laguz are back together, and very much in love. Everything is going to be okay now."

Gold nodded, but didn't look completely convinced. "You

did wonderful work, Emerald. Velvet and Laguz aren't the only Flames that you and Mica helped to reunite. The effect that you have had will ripple all across the world."

Emerald smiled, but she looked sad at the mention of Mica. "I'm not sure my own Flame is too pleased that I have chosen to return home. Perhaps I should have stayed there longer."

"As a matter of fact, I haven't yet asked you the ultimate question. Which I am sure you know well by now."

Emerald frowned. "I forgot that I can still change my mind if I wish to."

"It is possible to heal anything, you know that. So you could return, if that is your desire."

"I wish to stay," Emerald said, nodding her head. "I must have felt that it was important to leave at that point, there must be a reason for it. I have asked Velvet to take care of my Flame for me, I can only hope that he finds a way to continue without my presence."

Gold nodded. "I'm sure Velvet will do her best to look after him. Now, where would you like to go?"

"You know where I want to go, Gold. I want to go home."

"Very well." Gold stepped to one side so Emerald could pass. "Say hello to Pearl for me."

Emerald reached up to kiss him on the cheek as she passed by. "I will."

*   *   *

"When I woke up this morning, alone on the sofa, I thought that it had all been a long, weird dream," Reece said as she made coffee for herself and Leona. "Meeting you, then having to go home to watch my mother die, then coming back here, it all seemed so surreal."

Leona got up from her stool and wrapped her arms around her Flame. "I'm sorry I didn't stay with you on the sofa, my back was hurting, and I needed to stretch out."

Reece laughed. "Oh, I wasn't complaining about that, it was just that it was so odd, waking up on my sofa here, on my own in the apartment. I was quite relieved when I peeked into the bedroom to see you asleep in the bed."

"Are you feeling okay now? You must be pretty jet-lagged." Leona sat down again.

"Not too bad. Will feel better once I've had some of this." Reece served the coffee and took fresh croissants out of a box. Leona frowned.

"You already went out and got breakfast too?"

"I did." She joined Leona on the other side of the counter. They ate and drank in silence for a few minutes, and Leona couldn't remember the last time she had felt so contented. Suddenly, without warning, she was thrown into a vision.

She looked around her wildly, shocked at the suddenness and clarity of the vision. She was at her parents' house, sitting at the table. Her family were around her, eating dinner and chatting. She looked around for Reece, but she wasn't there.

"I'm so pleased to have you here, sweetie," her mother said to her. "I've missed you."

"Mum, there's something you should know," Leona said.

"What is it?"

"The thing is," Leona stalled, aware that all eyes were on her.

"Leona? Leona? Are you okay?"

Leona blinked and came back to the present moment. The curious eyes staring at her disappeared and she was back in the apartment in Paris, with a very worried lover in front of her.

"What just happened? I was talking to you, but you weren't here, your eyes were open but you couldn't see, I was calling you, but there was nothing."

Leona noticed that Reece was shaking, and she took her hands and held them still. "I'm so sorry. I should have explained this to you before. It's scary when you don't know what's happening, and I had forgotten that." She sighed. "I get visions. Visions of the future mostly. And when they come, it's like I'm somewhere else entirely."

Reece's eyebrows shot up. "Visions? Like, maybe of planes crashing?"

"What?" Leona was shocked. "How did you know about that?"

"There was a news report about it. They said some psychic saw a vision of the plane I was meant to be on crashing, and everyone dying. They said she stopped the plane taking off and identified the fault."

Leona remembered her vision of the news report, but she hadn't realised that the report had actually gone live after the incident. "Oh my goodness, I didn't know you knew."

"I didn't know you were the psychic! I didn't tell you about the report because I didn't want to scare you." Reece shook her head. "I can't believe it was you. You saw the plane crash? What happened?"

Tears sprang to Leona's eyes as she remembered the look on her beloved's face as the plane was going down. "It was awful," she whispered. "I saw it happen, and I knew that if I didn't do something, then I would never see you again."

Reece started to cry too, and she abandoned her food and threw her arms around Leona. "I'm here now, and I promise I will never leave you again."

Leona pulled back a little to kiss her. "I promise to never let you go."

Chapter Eleven

"Mike, it's time."

Violet's heart broke again at the sight of her Angel friend, struggling to knot his black tie. She went into the room to help him, and her eyes strayed to the bed where Esmeralda had died just the week before. She dragged her gaze away and focused on the soul before her who needed her to be strong for him in that moment. She undid the knot and started again, making sure that it looked straight.

"Thank you," Mike whispered. He shook his head. "I don't know how to do this, I don't know if I can."

"We'll do it together," Violet said, willing herself not to cry.

Mike nodded, not looking convinced. Violet squeezed his arm, then left the room, and he followed her downstairs, to where Greg was waiting. She had followed through on her promise to herself, and the house was now back to how Esmeralda had kept it, clean and tidy and in order. She picked up the bouquet of flowers they had chosen, took Greg's hand, and they went out to Mike's car. Greg got in the driver's seat and Violet sat in the back seat with Mike, her hand on his knee. They drove to the crematorium in silence, and when they got there, Violet gasped.

The small building was completely surrounded with people, and there were more arriving on foot. Greg drove through slowly, and the crowd parted for them. He pulled into the last remaining parking spot, and they got out of the car. Violet was overwhelmed by the number of people there, and was thrilled to see the familiar faces of her Spiritual Sisters among the crowd. She smiled at them, and they smiled back, tears already flowing.

Violet walked arm in arm with Mike, and held Greg's hand at the same time, feeling comforted with them either side of her. They waited in front of the building for the hearse to arrive, and when it did, Violet couldn't stop the tears that fell. The emerald green coffin that Mike had chosen was stunning, and was so perfect. Violet knew that Esmeralda would have approved. An angel wing made of white roses lay on top. Several men stepped forward to carry the coffin, and as it passed by them, Violet felt Mike slump next to her. She used all of her strength to support him. They followed the coffin into the crematorium, and sat in the front row, while everyone filed in behind them. Violet glanced around to see that the room was full to capacity, and that a large crowd of people stood outside the open doors.

Throughout the whole service, which was full of Esmeralda's favourite songs, and moving words from Earth Angels she had helped over the years, Mike sat with his head bowed. Violet held his hand tight, trying to channel strength and love toward him, but he seemed unable to move. When the service finished, and the coffin rolled away, past the curtain, Mike finally looked up to watch it go, and the tears began streaming down his face.

Greg squeezed Violet's other hand and she looked at him gratefully, while feeling guilty at the same time for being so thankful that her Flame still sat beside her. She could tell from his expression that Greg was feeling something similar. Somehow, they managed to get Mike back to the car, and they headed for the local pub, where Violet had arranged some food. She helped Mike inside, and found him a comfortable chair, which he slumped into. She went to the bar and got three glasses of whiskey. She didn't often drink much, but she felt the need for something stronger in that moment. She returned to Mike and Greg with the drinks, and the three of them toasted to Esmeralda. Soon, the pub filled up with some of those who had been at the service. Violet looked up and saw Amy, and excused herself to go and see her.

"Oh, Violet," Amy said, throwing her arms around the Old Soul. "I wish we were meeting up on a happier occasion."

"Me too, Angel, me too." Violet pulled back. "How are you?"

"I'm great, how is Mike doing?" Amy asked, looking over to where he sat.

"Not great. We literally arrived minutes before she died. He has been inconsolable since. Greg and I had to arrange most of this, he just hasn't been able to function."

"I'm not surprised. I mean, they're Flames, I saw what it did to you to lose Greg." Amy frowned then, wondering if she shouldn't have brought up such bad memories.

Violet sighed. "It's true. Losing a Twin Flame is not something that I ever want to experience again." She looked over at Greg, and he caught her gaze, as if he had heard her words. She smiled at him, and he nodded.

"How are things going with you two?"

Violet gestured for them to sit, and they nabbed a couple of chairs out of earshot of Greg. "It's going really well, though what with Leona being mistaken for a terrorist a few weeks back, and now Esmeralda leaving us, it's been quite a dramatic time."

"Leona? A terrorist? Are you serious?"

Violet shook her head. "Ridiculous, I know. She had a vision of a plane crashing, and then started screaming about it in the airport in Paris, not the most sensible thing to do."

"Wow, that's crazy. What happened? Did it crash?"

"No, luckily they grounded the plane, and she helped them

to identify the fault that was going to cause it to crash. She saved hundreds of lives, including the life of her own Twin Flame."

Amy sat back and exhaled loudly. "So life hasn't exactly been dull for you guys."

"I wish." Violet sipped her drink, and watched Mike for a bit. "I'm worried that he's not going to recover from this."

"All you can do is be there for him. He will find a way, like you found a way when you didn't think you would be with Greg again."

Violet frowned. That was the problem. Her way had included a twenty-year stint on the Other Side and then travelling back in time. Which probably wasn't an option for Mike.

Another familiar and welcome face came into Violet's vision, breaking her out of her thoughts.

"Maggie, it's so good to see you." She embraced her friend, who squeezed her tightly in return.

"Violet, my dear friend, are you okay?"

"I'm as good as you can be in these situations. It is a sad day for the world, to lose Esmeralda's light."

Maggie shook her head. "Oh, no, the world has not lost her light. Did you not see how many people were there to acknowledge her life and work? How many people she had helped? The ripples of the love she gave and the incredible work she did will continue to grow for a long time yet."

Violet smiled. "You are absolutely right. She told me that she had completed her most important mission, and that she was happy to go home. She will never be forgotten."

"I will drink to that." Keeley appeared with a round of fresh drinks, and Fay, Beattie and Leila appeared too. The Spiritual Sisters all took a glass, and toasted to Esmeralda, the Angel who had succeeded in reuniting so many Flames.

* * *

Theo watched them from a distance, staying out of sight as the small blonde woman danced along the pavement, hand in hand with the tall lanky owner of the Butterfly Zoo. He had no idea why he had taken to spying on the blonde, in fact he had no explanation for any of his crazy behaviour over the previous few weeks. All he knew was that he was single again because of it. And that he was still dreaming of Aria every night.

Crazy dreams of a million stars in the sky, and laying on a field of nothing but four-leafed clovers. Of flying side by side. Of sitting in a large theatre, or at the edge of a still lake, watching people's lives.

He was wondering if he should just go to the doctors and beg for medication. Because he was surely going mad.

Who was this woman? Where were these crazy dreams coming from? None of it made any sense to him. He watched them disappear around the corner, and he moved forward to his next post, to continue watching them. One thing he did know, was that he needed to speak to her soon. Before he got reported to the police for stalking. He really didn't want to get arrested. He watched then enter the zoo from a distance, and sighed. Would today be the day?

Suddenly, without any conscious thought, he found himself striding toward the entrance. If he didn't do something now, he would just turn into a crazed stalker. Or perhaps he already was one.

He entered the zoo, which was still in darkness, they hadn't opened properly or turned on the lights yet. He went straight to the staff door, and tried it. It was unlocked. He opened it and followed the corridor to the office. He opened the door without knocking, then jumped back when he saw Aria and Tim kissing each other passionately.

"Oh my god!" Aria squeaked when she opened her eyes and saw him. Tim stood in front of her protectively and frowned at Theo.

"What the hell are you doing? You can't just walk in here, what do you want?"

"The door was open," Theo said, waving his hand in the direction of the entrance. "I need to speak to Aria."

Aria frowned. "But you hate me. You wouldn't listen to me when I tried to talk to you weeks ago. Why now?"

"I keep dreaming of you. Of lakes, and theatres and eating chocolatey snacks with you."

Aria gasped, and her hand flew to her mouth. "You remember that?" she whispered.

"I don't know if they're memories, I just know that your face haunts me every night, and I think I might be going crazy."

Aria started to giggle, then she saw Tim's face and stopped. "Maybe we should talk," she said. She put her hand on Tim's arm. "We'll go and sit in the café if that's okay."

Tim frowned, and looked at Theo, then at Aria. But he didn't protest. "Just stay in the building."

Aria nodded, then she left the room, Theo trailing after her. She went to the café and made them both cups of tea. They sat down at one of the tables, and she stared at him like he was an exhibit in the zoo.

"Do you remember the Training Academy now? And the School for the Children?"

Theo shrugged. "I keep dreaming I'm in a building with white walls, and amazing gardens, and you. You are in every dream. I wake up thinking of you, wondering why you're not there."

Tears started falling down Aria's cheeks, even though she was smiling. "Tim said you might remember one day. But I had given up on that happening. I'm sorry I doubted you."

"So we were together? Before this life? In this white building, that was all real?"

Aria nodded. "It was all real. It's in the Fifth Dimension. I was a trainee at the Academy, and you were the assistant to the head, who was called-"

"Velvet. The lady with long grey hair. I remember her too."

Aria grinned. "Yes, Velvet. You do remember!" she exclaimed, unable to hide her pleasure. She frowned when Tim came out of the offices, and glanced their way as he switched on the lights and started the opening up process for the day. "I should get back to work," she said.

"I need to know more. Because I feel like I'm madly in love with you, and I don't know what to do about that. I mean, you're clearly in love with that Tim guy, and I was in love with Patty, but,"

"But what? Are you not with her anymore?" Aria sounded hopeful, and Theo smiled.

"No, she left me, because I was being so weird."

"Oh, I'm sorry," Aria said, not sounding in the least bit sorry about it.

"So what do we do now? Where do we go from here?"

Aria shook her head, and finished her drink. "I don't know, can you give me some time to figure it out? I love Tim, he has been amazing to me and has kept me going when things got dark, and I owe him so much. I can't just leave him…"

"I understand," Theo said, not really understanding at all. How could she love anyone else? In that moment, he knew with every atom of his being that they were meant to be together. And it was taking all his willpower and strength to not just pick her up and carry her out of there.

"Have you got a number? Once I know what to do I will call you," Aria said, taking their cups to the sink. She gave him a pen and a piece of till roll, and he scribbled his number on it. She tucked it into her pocket, and smiled at him. "I'll call you soon."

Theo nodded, realising that she was asking him to go. He stood up and backed away, aware that Tim was standing by the ticket desk, watching his every move.

"Bye," he said. He reached the door and he turned to leave.
"Bye," Aria echoed.

*   *   *

"I can't let you do that."

Ceri shook her head. "It's not your choice. It's mine. I don't care what happens today, I am marrying you."

Charlie stared into the eyes of his Flame and was overtaken by a feeling of wonder and bewilderment. How could this beautiful woman, so full of love and hope and promise, tie her future to his when his was going to be spent inside a cell? "What about your mum? I don't want to cause a rift between you, you will need her, and she needs you."

"My mum is happy with what I'm doing. She has given us her blessing."

Tears sprang to Charlie's eyes, and he reached out to hold her hand over the partition. Before he could speak, his lawyer was clearing his throat to get his attention, and the court was called to order.

"I love you," Ceri whispered.

"I love you too," Charlie replied, before turning to the front to face his fate.

"After considering all of the evidence, and past record, as well as testimonials from family and friends of both the defendant and the deceased, I have come to a decision on the sentencing," the judge said, looking up from his papers at the court. "I hereby sentence Charles Russell to ten years imprisonment for murder. With the possibility of parole after seven."

Charlie closed his eyes and his shoulders slumped. Though not as bad as it could have been, he had still hoped in vain for the sentence to be lighter. He wasn't even listening as the judge made his closing statements and dismissed them. He turned to look at Ceri, and she smiled encouragingly at him.

"I meant it. I am marrying you," she said. "I will make it happen." Not caring that he might be pulled away, Charlie leaned forward and she met him halfway. Their lips met for a few seconds before he was pulled away and led to his new home for the next ten years. But this time, it didn't seem like such a dark path. Because he had a bright light to accompany him along the way. He smiled at Ceri through his tears, and she waved.

*   *   *

"It occurred to me, that despite the fact we're having a child together, I really don't know very much about you," Gareth remarked as they shopped for baby clothes.

"What do you want to know?"

"Do you have any brothers or sisters? Where did you grow up? What do you want to do with your life? What's your favourite cupcake flavour?"

Starlight laughed at the last one, but her heart sank as she realised that she wouldn't be able to answer the first two questions. Because the truth would just scare him. She thought quickly.

"We have plenty of time to get to know each other yet, besides, you know that my favourite cupcake flavour is lemon curd."

Gareth smiled and squeezed her hand. "That's true. But seriously, I want to know everything about you, I want to know your fears, your hopes, your likes and dislikes. Everything."

Starlight frowned and grabbed the nearest item to her, which happened to be a baby grow with stars all over it. "I like this one, do you like this one? It's yellow, so it will be good for a girl or a boy. Do you think we should find out what the gender is when we can? It would certainly make all this easier."

Gareth looked at the baby grow and nodded, but he looked confused. He tugged on her hand so that she turned to face him. "What's wrong? Did I say something to upset you?"

Starlight shook her head. "No, it's just, I don't have any family. It's just me. I don't really remember growing up, and I'd really rather focus on the future, I don't want to talk about the past." All of what she said was true, but Starlight still felt guilty for omitting the truth, which was that she wasn't really human, and that she had no family or past because she had simply arrived here from the stars.

"I'm so sorry. I didn't know about your family." Gareth kissed her, and she closed her eyes, losing herself in his embrace. "I won't bring it up again, I promise."

Starlight smiled. "Thank you. Now then, do you like this one?"

"Yes, I do, I've always liked the stars. I studied astrology when I was younger."

"Really?" Starlight had to stop herself from laughing. "Do you still remember all of the constellations?"

They resumed walking down the aisle that contained an overwhelming range of baby-wear. "Most of them, though it's been a while since I got my telescope out. We'll have to get it out and have a look."

"I would like that. I would like that a lot."

They purchased the baby grow, and then headed out into the sunshine. Despite her initial reservations, Starlight was looking forward to the day that she would welcome a beautiful new soul into the world. She looked up then, and wondered if Gold was watching. As much as she missed him, she hoped that he wasn't. She hoped that he was busy helping souls on the Other Side, and not watching his Flame in the embrace of another man, having a child with him.

She tightened her grip on Gareth's hand and he smiled at her, and the warmth of his touch, his love, warmed Starlight to the core. She resolved to put Gold out of her mind, and to allow herself to be fully present with the man by her side. It was important. She wasn't sure why yet, but she knew she would find out in time.

*   *   *

"I'm a Mermaid!" Reece exclaimed, making Leona laugh. She shook the purple book at her. "It's right here, this description fits me to a T! Did you know I was a Mermaid?"

"Of course I did. But I wanted you to discover it for yourself."

Reece shook her head. "It just makes so much sense. I mean, I grew up near the water, was always on the beach, always swimming, and always had long hair, even though the salt water would tangle it, making it unbearably painful when my mum insisted on brushing it through."

Leona frowned. "How do you cope with being here? So far away from the water?"

"It's not easy. When I was back in Australia, I spent every moment that I wasn't with my mum at the beach. I hadn't realised just how much I missed it."

Leona was quiet for a while. She set her own book down. "Do you think you'll go back there?"

Reece understood the tone in her voice. It would be difficult to get Leona a permanent visa in Australia, because same-sex marriage wasn't legally recognised, and she didn't have a particular career that would make her eligible. "One day," she said. "Or I would at least like to move somewhere closer to the coast. It doesn't have to be Australia."

Leona relaxed a little. She picked up her book again, and Reece did the same, reading more about the other types of Earth Angels. After another twenty minutes, she put it down and sighed.

"What is it?" Leona asked.

"I've read nearly the whole book, and I cannot work out

which type you are. Because you don't fit into any of the categories fully. I mean, you have some Faerie qualities, but then you're really shy and quiet and not crazy and bouncing around. And I don't think you're an Angel, although you have saved my life at least once already. And I don't think you're a Mermaid. But I could be wrong?"

"I know I don't really fit into any of the categories easily, but I am an Elemental. I was a Faerie in my last life. But I was quiet, preferring to keep to myself." Leona played with her silver necklace as she spoke, and Reece smiled when she realised it was a Faerie.

"I didn't even notice you were wearing a Faerie the whole time!" Reece reached out to touch the pendant.

"My visions made me isolate myself from others, because I was afraid they would think I was weird. But I did make a friend, while I was at the Training Academy."

"Was that where you went to school?"

"In a way, yes. It was where you probably went, too. It's where the Angels, Faeries, Starpeople and Mermaids go to learn how to become human before being born here on Earth."

Reece shook her head. "How do you know all of this? It's amazing."

"I had a vision a few months ago that showed me some of it. And when I got the vision, I was in the process of picking up the seashell that's now in the bedroom. I kept it as a talisman. I knew that I would find you if I had it."

"This all just blows my mind a little. Have you met anyone else who know about this?"

"I have. I met Greg, who gave me this necklace, and I had visions of him meeting his Twin Flame, Violet. He saved her life when she fell off the rocks into the sea. Violet was the head of the Academy."

Reece's eyes widened. "Incredible. And they know? That they were together before?"

"I think they recognised each other very quickly. Just as

we recognised each other." Leona smiled and reached out to stroke Reece's cheek.

"I'm just in awe. It's like there's been a whole side of the world that I have just never noticed before. And you have opened my eyes to it. I'm so very thankful I followed my intuition and went for a drink in the train station."

"Me too. If I had left Paris and gone to Spain, who knows when or even if we might have met."

Reece shuddered. "It doesn't even bear thinking about. We're together now, that's the most important thing." She jumped up from the sofa suddenly, surprising Leona. "Let's get out of here and go somewhere. Have you explored much of Paris yet?"

"I'm embarrassed to say that I've never even been to the Eiffel Tower."

"We can't have that!" Reece held her hand out to Leona and pulled her to her feet.

About fifteen minutes later, armed with some snacks and a camera, the two women left the apartment and headed for the most iconic structure in Paris. They settled on the grass in front of it, and spent several minutes taking silly snapshots of each other, and laughing. Suddenly, Reece became serious.

"Leona."

Leona stopped laughing and frowned. "What?"

Without warning, Reece knelt down on one knee, and took a small box out of her pocket. Leona gasped when she opened the box to reveal a beautiful vintage engagement ring.

"This was my mother's legacy to me. And I know, without a doubt, that I want to spend the rest of my life with you, so will you please marry me?"

When Leona didn't respond for a moment, she waved her hand. "I know it's not actually legally recognised yet, but that doesn't matter, we can wait until it is. Because it will be soon, I know it. Just say you will be mine, always."

Leona couldn't help a tear trickling down her cheek at her

words. She smiled and nodded. "Yes, I will be yours. And I will marry you. The moment it is possible to do so."

Reece took her left hand, removed the ring from the box and slid it onto her finger. They were both surprised when it fit perfectly.

Reece smiled at Leona, who pulled her up from the ground. They kissed deeply, and Leona melted into her arms. When they pulled away, they both started giggling again. Reece looked around, and called out to a passer-by.

"Excusez-moi?"

"Oui?" the man responded.

"Could you take a photo of me and my fiancée?" Reece asked in prefect French. He nodded and came over to them. She handed him the camera, and they posed in front of the tower, and he kept snapping away while they laughed, kissed and Leona held out her hand with the ring sparkling in the sunlight.

Finally, they thanked the kind man and he returned the camera then went on his way.

"I will never forget this moment," Reece whispered into Leona's ear.

"Me either."

Chapter Twelve

"Do you think we will be able to leave soon?"

Violet looked over at Greg, who was lying next to her, staring at the ceiling of the guest room. She put her book down and snuggled into his side. "I don't know. Every time I think Mike is making progress, and moving on, something happens to knock him down again."

Greg nodded. Just the previous day, the mail had brought with it a letter addressed to Esmeralda, from a lady who had met her Twin Flame after attending the retreat. Mike had read the letter, and spent the whole day sitting outside by the pond and crying.

"I don't want to be insensitive, I completely understand his devastation, but we've been here for six months now. We've been running this place for Mike, which has been amazing, but at some point we will need to move on, and Mike will have to decide what he wants to do, whether to keep running the retreat or not."

"You're right. We can't stay here forever, but I did promise Esmeralda that I would make sure Mike was okay. Besides, I love being here, you can almost forget there's a whole world out there, when you're enclosed in these woods."

"I love it too. And I know that what we're doing is important. More people need to find their Flames. I get that, I do."

"But we have our own missions, I know."

Greg nodded. "Though I'm not a hundred percent certain what mine is anymore."

"And you think I know what mine is?" Violet laughed.

"Of course. You're going to write books. And your words will inspire millions of Earth Angels." The words were out of Greg's mouth before he thought them through.

Violet frowned and sat up to look at Greg properly. "Where did that come from? I'm not a writer."

Greg shook his head. "I don't know, I just always had a feeling that was what you were meant to do."

"Huh. I do like writing, but I've only ever written in my diary, and the occasional poem. What makes you think I could write books?"

"Just a feeling." Greg pulled her back down next to him, and she rested her head on his chest. "Give it a try. Write about us, about your Earth Angel friends, about the Twin Flames. Who knows where it might take you?"

A couple of hours later, Greg and Violet were sat with the participants of the weekend retreat that was in progress, doing the same meditation that Violet and Amy had done with Esmeralda and Mike, so long ago. It made Violet feel sad that Esmeralda wasn't there to lead the meditation, but she thought that Greg did it well. Mike had bowed out of the session, and had gone into town to get more food. She was trying to concentrate on Greg's words, but her worry over Mike, and her curiosity over Greg's idea of writing books was distracting her from the present moment.

"In front of you, there will be a wall with lots of different coloured and shaped doors on it. Find the door with your name on it, and then step through it, to a moment in the past where you might have met your Twin Flame."

Violet focused and saw in front of her a familiar ornate purple door, bearing her name. She smiled and pushed the door open, then found herself in a white corridor. She looked down and saw she was clothed in purple velvet robes. She realised she was back at the Academy. She looked back at the door she had stepped through, and it said 'Main Hall - Backstage'. The moment felt familiar, and she frowned.

A blur of silvery black came into her vision, and she was pulled into a tight embrace. After a moment, she stepped back and looked up at the face of Mike.

"Mica! What was that for?"

Mike grinned. "I've been called! I wanted to tell you this morning, but class was cancelled. So I thought I would wait here to tell you. You don't mind if I don't stay for this session do you? Only the quicker I go the less of an age difference there will be between Emerald and I."

Violet laughed and shook her head. "Of course I don't mind!" She pulled Mike back into another hug. "I'm so, so happy for you, Mica. I knew the two of you would be together. There's only a couple of years between you, I'm sure it won't keep you apart." She pulled back again and smiled warmly at the Angel.

"I hope you, too, are reunited with your Flame."

Violet nodded. "Thank you. Now go. Get to Earth, find Emerald and help as many souls find their Twin Flames as possible."

Mike grinned and did a mock salute. "Yes, Ma'am."

Violet laughed and he disappeared. "Bye, Mica," she said, still smiling. She opened the door to the main hall, and found herself back in the corridor of doors. She snapped back to the present moment, and the meaning of the memory she had just experienced became clear. She forced her eyes open and leaned over to Greg.

"Greg," she whispered urgently. He opened his eyes and looked at her, surprised she was interrupting the meditation, he looked around, but the others in the group seemed undisturbed.

"What?" he asked.

"Mike's in trouble. I have to go, you stay here."

"What? How do you know? Shall I come with you?"

Violet shook her head and leaned over to kiss him. "I'll take my phone and keep in touch, you look after everyone here." She got up and left the tent, as quickly and quietly as she could. She ran over to the house and retrieved her phone and the camper-van keys. Then she ran out of the house and down the lane to where the van was parked.

It took a couple of tries to start it as it had been sitting there unused for some time. She was driving down the lane before she started shivering and the reality of the situation started sinking in. She kept going, following her intuition that told her to head to the nearest main road. When she got to the dual carriageway, and she heard the sirens of the emergency vehicles approaching from behind her, she knew that what she feared was true. The ambulance and police overtook her, and it wasn't much further down the road before she got stuck in the standstill traffic. Not caring that it might be dangerous, she switched on the camper-van hazard lights, and switched off the engine. She grabbed her phone, got out, and ran down the side of the road, past the cars, toward the blue flashing lights. When she saw the overturned car, and the lorry that was sideways in the road, her thudding heart stalled. It was Mike's car.

She ran over toward it, and was stopped by a police officer.

"Hey, you can't go near there."

"That's my friend," she gasped. "Mike, in the car."

The officer didn't let her go, but he relaxed his grip a little. "We're waiting for the fire service, we can't get him out, but the paramedics are assisting him as best they can."

Violet watched the paramedics working around the crumpled metal, and tears began streaming down her cheeks. "He's still alive?"

"Yes, but he has some pretty severe injuries as far as we

can see." The officer sighed and made her turn away from the scene. "He's unconscious and not responding. But I promise that we are doing our best to help him."

Violet nodded, and heard more sirens approaching. "You can let go now," she said, straightening up a little. The officer nodded and let go, and she wobbled a bit on her feet. He put his hand on her arm to steady her and she smiled at him gratefully. She watched the fire engine pull up, and the firemen jump out and set to work, freeing Mike from the wreckage. The sound of the metal crunching made her wince, and she prayed hard to the Angels that he would be okay. A vibration in her hand made her look down at her forgotten phone, and she saw that Greg was calling. She pressed the green button and put it to her ear.

"Violet? Are you okay? What's going on? Did you find Mike?"

Violet sighed and explained what had happened, having to raise her voice over the noise. While they spoke, Violet saw that they were taking Mike from the car and she told Greg that she would call him back. She approached slowly, staying out of the way of the professionals. When they lay him on the stretcher, her heart sank at the sight of him. He was covered in blood and glass and wasn't moving. At all.

There was a flurry of activity as they started to try and resuscitate him, but Violet already knew that it was too late.

He had already gone home to Esmeralda.

*   *   *

"It's time, isn't it?"

Aria sighed and nodded. "I'm so sorry, Tim, but I don't think I can do this anymore."

"I know. I think I knew six months ago when Theo started to remember he was Linen. I knew then that you wouldn't stay with me." Tim put his fork down and sighed. "I'm sorry that

I've stopped you from being together, it was wrong of me."

Aria got up and went around the table to him. "Don't be silly. You didn't stop me, I chose to stay here, because I love you. You're my best friend, Tim."

Tim looked at her and shook his head. "But it's not enough. You belong with him." He tried to smile. "You don't want to be stuck with a boring old alien like me."

Aria frowned. "You're not boring at all. I have a lot of fun when I'm with you, and you took me in, and took care of me, and-"

"And I promised that no matter what, we would remain friends. You shouldn't stay because I gave you a job and somewhere to live. You need to be true to yourself. Because I can see that you haven't been, and it's making you lose your sparkle."

They were both quiet for a while until Tim spoke. "Have you talked to him recently?"

"He called me yesterday," Aria admitted. "We talked for a couple of hours."

Tim nodded. "As much as I want you to stay, I understand that you need to go."

"I do love you, Tim."

"I love you too, Aria. Which is why I am letting you go."

Tears streaming down her cheeks, Aria leaned forward to kiss her best friend. "Friends forever?"

Tim nodded, tears welling up in his own eyes. "Now go. Your Flame is waiting for you."

An hour later, Aria had piled all of her belongings by the door, and was just having a hug with Tim when there was a knock at the door. Tim went to open it before Aria could stop him, and he opened the door to find Theo waiting there. He held out his hand and Theo shook it.

"Take good care of her. Otherwise you will have me to answer to."

Theo nodded. "I promise I will."

"Good." Tim walked away, and went to his room, closing the door behind him.

"Is he okay?" Theo asked Aria.

"I hope he will be," she replied. She picked up one of her bags and Theo picked up the other two.

"This everything?"

Aria nodded, then put her set of keys on the side table before stepping out of the door, closing it behind her.

She followed Theo to the car he'd borrowed, and they put her bags in the back. Before she could climb in, he pulled her into his arms and looked into her eyes, which were lit up by the moonlight.

"Are you sure about this?" he whispered. "You look so sad."

"Of course I'm sure. I love Tim, but he's not my Flame. You are. We came here together, we are meant to be together." She kissed him. "I love you, Linen."

Theo smiled. "I guess I might have to change my name then. You don't like Theo?"

Aria shook her head. "No, you don't look like a Theo."

He laughed and released her, and they bantered all the way to their new home together.

*   *   *

It had taken several months of planning, but the day had finally arrived, and Charlie was nervously waiting at the front of the prison chapel, for his Flame. He had tried several times to convince her to think about it for longer, after all, they had more than enough time to wait and think it over – what if she met someone else? He didn't want to tie her down and be a burden to her.

But she was insistent. She wanted to marry him and she wanted to do it as soon as possible.

Charlie glanced to the side, where his mum sat, and she

smiled at him encouragingly. Despite everything, she had stuck with him and supported him through the whole ordeal, and he was so thankful for her.

The music started, and Charlie turned to look down the aisle. Walking toward him was the most beautiful soul he had ever seen. Dressed in an understated cream dress, holding a small bouquet of bright pink flowers; Ceri walked toward him, a huge smile on her face. Her mother walked alongside her, taking the place of her father.

The father that Charlie had murdered.

Charlie's heart thudded and his chest tightened and he found himself gasping for breath. How could he go through this? How could Ceri want this? How could her mother be happy that her daughter was marrying the man who had killed her husband? It was all just so surreal that he couldn't even begin to make sense of it.

He felt a nudge, and he looked at the guard stood next to him, who was acting as his best man.

"Breathe," he whispered.

Charlie nodded, and drew in deep, ragged breaths. A few seconds later, Ceri stood by his side, and the proximity of her beauty melted all of his doubts and worries away.

He loved her to the very depths of his being, throughout every part of his soul. It was going to hurt, spending years away from her, confined to these prison walls, but he would do his best to make sure that she never felt alone.

The ceremony seemed to be over in a flash, and before he knew it, they were married.

He leaned in to kiss her, and he lingered for as long as he could, taking in her scent, her warmth, her lips on his. They were allowed a drink afterwards, for their wedding reception, and his mum snapped some photos, but all too soon, their time was up, and Charlie had to return to his cell.

"When I get out of here, we will have the most amazing honeymoon, I promise."

Ceri smiled, and kissed him one last time. "I'll hold you to that," she teased. "Do I get to choose where?"

"Absolutely. Anywhere you want to go, I'll take you. That's a promise."

"I look forward to it."

Charlie allowed himself to be led away then, thankful that the guard didn't cuff him until they stepped out of the room. He went back to his cell, and slumped onto his bed. He knew that as long as he could keep the memory of Ceri's smile in his mind, then he could get through the next few years, no matter what happened.

Not bothering to change out of the suit his mum had brought him, he lay back on the lumpy mattress, and closed his eyes. He replayed every moment of the day, determined not to forget a single second.

*   *   *

"Mica! You have come to find Emerald, I presume?"

Mica smiled at Gold. "Yes, Gold. There was just no way I could continue on Earth without her. We just cannot be apart, it's not possible."

Gold sighed. "I completely understand, my dear Angel. Twin Flames should indeed be together. I won't even bother to ask you the question."

"I am staying here. Or, rather, I will go home to the Angelic Realm, I assume that is where Emerald is?"

"You assume right. I need a word with Pearl, so I will accompany you there." Gold looked at the Indigo Child. "You will be okay while I am gone?"

She nodded. "Of course."

Mica and Gold set off toward the gates to the Angelic Realm, and within moments, they saw Pearl there. She welcomed them both, and embraced Mica.

"Welcome home, Mica! Emerald has been waiting for

you." She gestured for him to enter and the gates opened. Before he could set one foot inside, he heard his name being called, and there was a blur of green rushing toward him.

"Mica!" Emerald threw herself into his arms, and kissed him all over.

He laughed, pleased to see her looking so healthy and vibrant again. He kissed her back. "Oh, Emerald. I missed you so much! I just couldn't do it without you. Velvet tried her best, but I just had to come home to you."

Emerald looked into his eyes, an understanding smile on her face. "I know, my love. I am so sorry that I left you, and that you had to leave Earth in such a way. I wish it had been a more peaceful passing."

Mica shrugged. "I felt no pain. I think I left my body pretty quickly. Anyway, none of that matters, all that matters is that I have found you again." He smiled and held out his arm. "Shall we?"

Emerald took his arm and Gold and Pearl watched them walk down the path toward the lake. Gold sighed and touched the rune pendant hung around his neck. Pearl smiled at him.

"It is hard for you to see Twin Flames reuniting when yours is not with you, I know."

"Yes. But I am pleased for them, all the same. I wouldn't wish this feeling of loneliness and despair on anyone."

Pearl touched his arm gently. "Gold, you are never alone, surely you of all people must know that. Why have you disconnected? I told you before that Starlight is within you at all times."

"I know. I do not know why this melancholy has gripped me so in this way."

"Yes, you do."

Gold frowned at Pearl. "Remind me?"

"It's because you have allowed it to grip you. You have welcomed the darkness in. Because truly that is the only way it can affect you in this way; with your invitation for it to do so. You could choose, in an instant, to stop letting it affect you, to have no impact on you, and it would be so."

"You are of course right."

Pearl smiled. "Being right doesn't matter. All that matters is if you take that information and do something with it. You can decide to stop wasting your energy on melancholy, and focus on the good instead."

Gold nodded, but didn't comment. He knew he had allowed his broken heart to affect him deeply and to take over his entire existence. Which wasn't helping anyone. Not Starlight, not the souls that he helped across, not the Indigo Child, and not himself.

"Thank you, Pearl. Your wisdom is most appreciated as always."

"You're welcome, Gold. You know where I am if you are in need of more."

Gold thought for a moment, then he reached behind his head and untied the cord around his neck. He placed the wooden pendant in Pearl's hands, who then closed her fingers around it.

She smiled, but said nothing.

Gold patted her hands thankfully, then headed off into the mist. He straightened his shoulders and walked more upright, as he made the decision that it was time to let go of his sadness, and focus on being of service. By the time he reached the Indigo Child, he felt as though a massive weight had lifted from him. And judging by the smile the Child gave him as he approached, he knew she could sense it too.

*   *   *

"Do you think it's possible to be any happier?" Reece said, sighing in contentment.

Leona smiled at her across the kitchen counter. "I don't think it is. This is happiest that I've ever been in my life, but,"

Reece was grinning up to the last word. "But what?" she said, a frown replacing her smile.

"I need to figure out what I'm doing. My travel fund is running low, and there is nothing to replenish it with. I need some employment, as quickly as possible."

Reece's frown smoothed out and she nodded. "Okay, that's cool. I could ask at work if there's anything going if you want me to."

Leona frowned. "I don't think I'd make a good English teacher. My grammar and punctuation are awful. No, I think I'll look for something less skilled than that. Maybe some waitressing or retail work. There must be some shops and cafés that would appreciate an English speaker?"

"You would have thought so," Reece agreed.

"I'm going to go out this afternoon and start looking. Are you working today?"

Reece nodded then looked at the clock. "Oops! I better go." She finished the rest of her coffee, then dashed around the counter to kiss Leona quickly. Then she grabbed her bag and coat and ran out the door.

"See you later," Leona called out. The door closed and Leona sighed. Despite her outward confidence, the idea of searching for work in Paris filled her with dread.

She delayed as long as she could, and changed her outfit four times before finally settling on one. She left the apartment and set off down the street, forcing herself to walk confidently and breathe deeply. She wasn't sure why she felt so nervous, but something just felt a little off.

Four cafés, two restaurants and three shops later, the feeling of dread had taken up camp in Leona's stomach. No one wanted an English girl with broken French. Not even to wash pots or sweep floors. She decided to go for a walk along the river, and just as she reached the water's edge, she was thrown into a vision.

"It won't be for long. We'll be back together before you

know it." Leona looked into Reece's eyes, which were red and puffy from crying.

"You don't have to go, we can figure something out. Or I can come with you to England."

Leona felt herself shaking her head. "You have a really good job here, and my old job pays enough that I'll be able to visit for long weekends."

"I hate this."

Leona's heart broke, and she pulled Reece into a kiss. "I hate it too, but I need to earn some money, and I'm just not getting anywhere here."

"I know," Reece whispered. "It just doesn't feel like we've had enough time together."

"I'll be back as soon as I can. If I work and save it all for six months, I'll be able to come back and be with you again."

Reece tried to smile, but didn't manage to pull it off. "Call me when you get there. I love you."

"I will, and I love you too." She hugged Reece again, before she picked up her rucksack and headed for the train. She looked back once just before boarding to see Reece standing there, watching her leave, tears streaming down her face.

"Excusez-moi?"

Leona snapped back to the present and looked at the old man in front of her. "Sorry?" she said.

"Oh good, you're English. Do you know which way I go to get to the Louvre?"

Pleased that for once, her English was actually of use to someone, she directed the man to the museum, then found a bench by the river to sit down. She needed a moment to process her vision. If felt like it would be coming soon, and it scared her. Leave Reece and go back to her old job? Go back to England? She shuddered at the idea, but at the same time, her job hunting had been a complete disaster, so it wasn't a far-fetched solution. She knew that her old boss would have her back there in a flash.

She sighed. Part of her wanted to fight against it, to step up the job hunting and really go for it, change the vision of the future she had Seen. But a stronger part of her knew that if she had Seen it, then it was bound to happen, after all, her visions never lied to her.

Leona frowned. Except for the plane crash. She had changed that future. She had stopped the plane from crashing. She had changed Reece's fate, and in turn, changed her own. She sat up straight. But changing it required action. Definitive action, with conviction and passion behind it. She had done whatever it took to save Reece's life, so why couldn't she do whatever it took to keep them together?

With that thought in mind, Leona jumped up and marched back to the apartment. She needed to get on the internet and find local French classes. If learning the language was what it would take to be able to stay and get a job, then that was what she would do.

Chapter Thirteen

Violet couldn't stop crying, and Greg felt helpless about it. He placed a cup of tea in front of her, where she sat on the sofa bundled up in a blanket. He sat next to her and wrapped his arms around her tightly.

"I've sorted out the cancellations," he said, for lack of anything comforting to say. "I've cleared the bookings for the next two weeks. We'll have to work out what will happen after that."

Violet nodded, but she didn't speak. She stared down at the shredded tissue in her hands. "I just can't get the image of Mike out of my mind. He was just, broken." A sob escaped and as she tried to breathe deeply, her body shuddered.

"I should have left the meditation and come with you, I just had no idea what you were heading for."

"Neither did I, I just knew that he was in trouble."

"What did you see? In the meditation?"

Violet described her memory. "It was when Emerald had already left for Earth, and Mica was worried he wouldn't find her, and was desperate to leave the Academy and get to Earth. I knew, when I had that memory, that it was Mike's soul's way of telling me he was leaving Earth."

Greg shook his head. "Incredible. We really are all so very connected, aren't we?"

Violet nodded. "The thing is, I know that he is with

Esmeralda now, and is happy again. Her death just destroyed him, and it was awful to watch him like that. But what will happen to the Twin Flame Retreat? To all they have built here? This place is needed in the world. They were needed in the world." Violet's voice broke and her body shuddered again. Greg tightened his grip on her and kissed her on the side of her head.

"Perhaps they have done all they could do. Perhaps it was time for them to help us all from the Other Side."

"Perhaps," Violet agreed softly. "It just makes me sad."

"Me too. They were amazing Angels, and they were very much loved." Greg paused for a moment, unsure whether it was too soon to bring up the subject. "Do you think Mike's family will take care of the funeral?"

Violet shook her head. "I don't know. I don't even know if I can handle another funeral so soon."

Greg sighed. "I know. But it will be good to celebrate Mike's life, and all the amazing things he did. I was thinking, he'd probably like his ashes scattered in the garden here, where he scattered Esmeralda's."

"Yes, that's a lovely idea. I think you're right." Violet was quiet for a moment, then she looked at Greg. "Do you think that we would go like that? Quickly, one after the other?"

Greg pulled her tighter to him, and a vision of being on the beach, a ragged piece of notepaper in his hands and Amy sat next to him went through his mind. "Let's not think about it. We're here, we're together. And that's all that matters." His voice lowered. "But I know I would find it difficult to be here, without you."

Violet's shoulders shook as she tried not to cry. "I would too."

Greg sighed. "Do you want to go for a walk? Get some fresh air? It's not good being stuck inside like this."

Violet nodded. "Yes, I would like that. I'll go get changed."

A few minutes later, they headed out of the door, and hand in hand, set off down the path into the woods. "I know a few days ago I was keen to leave, but I must admit, I will miss this place when we go."

"Me too. I hope that it stays as it is now, that Mike and Esmeralda's family sell it to someone that keeps the retreat going."

"It would be a shame to see it close."

"I've been thinking about what you said," Violet said, carefully stepping over some loose rocks. "About me writing books. I had an idea, to write about Earth Angels and how they attended the Training Academy before they came here."

Greg smiled, pleased that Violet had taken him seriously. "I think that sounds like a great idea. That way, they will remember their lives as Elementals and Angels and will wake up."

"That would be the idea. But I think I should write it in story form. I think if I wrote it as a memoir I would get locked up."

Greg chuckled, and Violet smiled for the first time in days. "That's true. If you start telling people you believe in Faeries and aliens, they'll either think you're on drugs or mentally unstable."

"Or both," Violet said.

"So when are you going to start writing it?"

Violet shrugged. "I might start scribbling down some ideas. I have some notes on the Academy in my diary from my meditations, I could use those as references."

"Sounds like a plan. It will be good to have a project. I just need to work out what my purpose is now."

"Maybe your purpose is to love me."

Greg pulled Violet toward him for a kiss. "Maybe it is."

*   *   *

"So what is the grand plan?"

Linen raised an eyebrow. "The grand plan? What do you mean?"

Aria set her mug down and tilted her head to one side. "Well, we decided to come to Earth, and find each other, so we could be a part of the Awakening, and hopefully be a part of the Golden Age. So far, we have regained our memories and have found each other, which I think is pretty amazing. Now we need to work out what happens next."

"Did we figure any of this out on the Other Side? Did we have a plan that I have forgotten about?"

Aria frowned and drank some more tea. "I don't think so, but then I don't remember every single little thing from the Other Side, so it's possible."

They were both quiet for a while and continued eating breakfast. After a few minutes, Aria shrugged. "Whether we planned something before or not, we need a plan now. Otherwise we might just fall asleep again, and we can't have that."

Linen swallowed some toast and frowned. "I don't think that would actually be possible. I can't imagine you falling asleep and forgetting all of this."

Aria giggled. "That's true. Don't you think it's funny that on the Other Side, I was convinced that I would be the only one who wouldn't be able to remember anything? But I remember loads! It took Velvet ages to remember and wake up, and Laguz took several tries to wake up too!"

"You are a very clever Faerie," Linen said seriously.

Aria smiled. "You've told me that before, I think."

Linen leaned over and kissed her softly. "That's because it's true. The way you see things, the way you link things up and make sense of them is amazing."

"I think we need to find some of Amethyst's books, and maybe even do some courses or something, and then help people wake up that way. I loved working in the Butterfly Zoo, because it was like being at home, but I think the whole point of us being here, on Earth right now, is to really experience being here, not to escape to somewhere more fun."

"That sounds reasonable enough. My job is just a job, it's not something I love doing. Playing the piano in the pub is fun though."

Aria frowned. "How did you even remember what your job was? I don't have any memories from the person's life who owned this body before me."

"I don't know, the body must have retained some of the memories because I knew my name and where I worked and how to do my job. But you said you didn't?"

"Not at all. Hadn't got a clue who I was, who my family were or what was going on. All I knew was my body was crazy heavy, and my wings had gone."

Linen chuckled at Aria's pout. "Maybe that's why you remember before more easily than me. You didn't have memories that weren't your own crowding them out."

"Maybe. Anyway, so shall we look up those courses?"

"Now?"

"Now is all that exists. So let's make the most of it."

*   *   *

"I brought you something," Ceri said. "I left it at the front desk, they said they'd give it to you once it had been checked out."

"Thank you. How is your mum?"

"She's good. She's like a different person. She's been meeting up with old friends, ones that Dad had scared away, and she's even looking to get a job, because he never allowed her to work, either."

Charlie nodded. "That's good."

"Yes." Ceri sighed. "I hate that you are in here, I hate the way things happened, but I cannot deny the fact that Dad's death has released us. And though it seems so wrong to be grateful, because you are paying the price for our freedom with yours, I really am thankful."

A tear caught Charlie by surprise as it made its way down his cheek. "Hearing that makes being here, makes being apart from you, bearable. Although," Charlie paused as a thought occurred to him, but he was afraid to voice it.

"Although what?"

"You didn't just marry me because you felt bad that I am in prison for doing something that you wanted to happen? Out of guilt or something?"

Ceri laughed. "Of course not, don't be silly. I married you because I love you so much, and I wanted you to know that I will wait, for as long as it takes, to be with you again."

Charlie smiled. "I'm sorry for doubting your intentions. This place just makes you a little crazy. Too much time to think."

"I understand," Ceri said softly. The bell rang then, signalling the end of the visiting session. "Our time is always too short."

"I wish you could stay longer too."

"I'll see you next week," Ceri said, getting to her feet and slipping her coat on. "I love you."

"I love you too."

He watched her go, then got up to be cuffed and led back to his cell. A couple of hours later, there was a tap at the door, and Charlie jumped up to receive the envelope that Ceri had brought him. He sat down on the chair and opened it up, to find a photograph inside. It was of him and Ceri on their wedding day, and they were beaming at the camera, their bodies entwined. He studied Ceri's face, and saw nothing but love and hope and joy. He flipped the photo over, and read Ceri's words.

Happiest day of my life, I love you, Ceri. xxx

Charlie smiled, then he propped the photo up on his

bedside table. No matter what, he would hold her in his arms again, as a free man. He wouldn't give up until he did.

*   *   *

Starlight stroked her growing belly and smiled when she felt a tiny foot kicking within her. She was loving being pregnant. Despite being the Angel of Destiny for aeons, and being the caretaker of the universe, the idea of actually giving birth to another being, caring for and nurturing a new soul, was exciting.

She smiled up at Gareth as he handed her a glass of water before sitting down next to her. He pressed the play button and they continued watching City of Angels. Though it was an older movie, Starlight had chosen it because she loved the idea of an Angel becoming human to be with the one they loved.

When the end credits rolled, Starlight was so glad to have Gareth next to her, firmly holding her hand and passing her some tissues.

"Are you okay?" he whispered. At this point, he was used to her being emotional at the drop of a hat, but he was still concerned, nonetheless.

"Yes," Starlight blew her nose then sniffled. "I just really wanted them to have more time together. It always seems so cruel when two people who love each other so deeply get to spend so little time together." She thought of her sister and her Twin Flame, and wondered if they had stayed together since their reunion. She hoped so. The world needed their love in order to experience the Golden Age. She looked forward to meeting her sister again, and knew that it would happen soon, and that together they would Awaken the Earth Angels. But until then, she was going to enjoy becoming a mother, and being with her soulmate.

She only hoped that Gold was happy, and that he would still be waiting for her when she got home.

"Feeling better?" Gareth asked.

Starlight nodded. "Yes, thank you." She leaned over to kiss him, and let go of all her worries. "Much better now."

*   *   *

"I have a job!"

Reece ran over to Leona and engulfed her in a hug. "Well done! That's amazing! Where?"

Leona laughed. "At the language centre. I went in to find out about French classes, and they were in need of an admin assistant who could speak English! So I applied, and they've said yes! They'll even throw in the French classes I wanted to do for free."

Reece shook her head with a smile. "That's incredible! Well done, I'm so proud of you." She kissed Leona, and Leona responded, deepening the kiss. Before either of them knew it, they had undressed each other and were heading for the bedroom. When they surfaced an hour later, they sat in the lounge, wrapped in dressing downs and sipping champagne.

"This champagne is amazing, but are you sure we should have opened it?"

Reece waved her hand dismissively. "I have a bottle given to me by a friend every year, and I never drink them. So it's nice to have something to celebrate and someone to drink them with!" She smiled. "So when do you start?"

"The job starts on Monday. I will have some training during the first week, my French class starts the week after on the Wednesday evening."

"That's brilliant. I can't believe it happened so quickly."

"Me neither. I'm just so relieved I can stay now."

Reece frowned. "Stay? Where were you going?"

Leona explained the vision to her, and her revelation afterwards that she should be able to change her fate, if she was able to stop the plane from crashing.

"Wow. So have you definitely changed your fate? Because I don't like the sound of that vision at all." Reece squeezed Leona's hand. "I never want to have to say goodbye to you ever again."

"I hope so. I hope that by getting a job here that pays enough, I have taken away the need for me to return to the UK. But I haven't had any further visions to confirm that I have changed my future."

With those words, Reece and the lounge disappeared, and Leona found herself walking down the aisle of a small room, toward a beautiful woman with red hair, in a white dress. She smiled at the friends and family she passed, until she reached the front. She took the hand of the beautiful red-haired woman, then together they turned to face the front and the ceremony began.

She blinked and came back to the present, then smiled at the beautiful woman beside her.

"I have changed my fate, and yours. We won't have to say goodbye now."

"I'll drink to that," Reece said, clinking her champagne glass against Leona's. "Here's to being together forever," she said.

"Forever," Leona agreed.

About the Author

Michelle lives in England, and when not writing and publishing her own books, she helps other Indie Authors with their own publishing adventures. She has known all her life that she is a writer. It is more of a calling than simply a passion, and despite her attempts to live in the normal world, she has finally realised that she would much rather live in a world full of magic and mystery.

Please feel free to write a review of this book on **Amazon**, or even just click the Like button. Michelle loves to get direct feedback, so if you would like to contact her, please e-mail theamethystangel@hotmail.co.uk or keep up to date by following her blog – **twinflameblog.com.** You can also follow her on Twitter **@themiraclemuse** or 'like' her page on **Facebook.**

To sign up to her mailing list for monthly newsletters, visit: **michellegordon.co.uk**

The Earth Angel Series:

The Earth Angel Training Academy (book 1)

Velvet is an Old Soul, and the Head of the Earth Angel Training Academy on the Other Side. Her mission is to train and send Angels, Faeries, Merpeople and Starpeople to Earth to Awaken the humans.

The dramatic shift in consciousness on Earth means that the Golden Age is now a possibility. But it will only happen if the Twin Flames are reunited, and the Indigo, Crystal and Rainbow Children come to Earth, to spread their love, light and wisdom.

While dealing with all the many changes, Velvet struggles to see the bigger picture. When she is reunited with her Flame for the first time in many lifetimes, her determination and resolve to fulfil her mission falter...

The Earth Angel Awakening (book 2)

'No matter how overcast the sky, the stars continue to shine. We just have to be patient enough to wait for clouds to lift.'

Twenty-five years after leaving the Earth Angel Training Academy to be born on Earth as a human, Velvet (now known on Earth as Violet) is beginning to Awaken. But when she repeatedly ignores her dreams and intuition, she misses the opportunity to be with her Twin Flame, Laguz. Without the long-awaited reunion with her Twin Flame, can Violet possibly Awaken fully, and help to bring the world into the elusive Golden Age?

The Other Side (of The Earth Angel Training Academy)

Mikey is an ordinary boy who just happens to talk to the Faeries at the bottom of his garden. So when an Angel visits him in his dream and tells him he must return to the Earth Angel Training Academy in order to save the world, despite his fears, he understands and accepts the task.

Starlight is the Angel of Destiny. By carefully orchestrating events at the Academy and on Earth, she can make sure that everything works out the way that it should, even though it may not make sense to those around her.

Leon is a Faerie Seer. He arrives at the Academy as a trainee, but through his visions he realises that his role in the Awakening is far more important than he ever imagined.

Visionary Collection:

Heaven dot com

When Christina goes into hospital for the final time, and knows that she is about to lose her battle with cancer, she asks her boyfriend, James, to help her deliver messages to her family and friends after she has gone.

She also asks him to do something for her, but she dies before he can make it happen, and he finds it difficult to forgive himself.

After her death, her messages are received by her loved ones, and the impact her words have will change their lives forever.

The Doorway to PAM

Natalie is an ordinary girl who has lost her way. There is nothing particularly special about her or her life. She has no exceptional abilities. She hasn't achieved anything miraculous. Her life has very little meaning to it.

Evelyn is the caretaker at Pam's. The alternate dimension where souls at their lowest point find the answers they need to turn their lives around. The dimension dreamers visit, to help people while they sleep.

One ordinary girl, one extraordinary woman.
One fated meeting that will change lives.

The Elphite

Ellie's life is just one long, bad case of déjà vu. She has lived her life before - a hundred times before - and she remembers each and every lifetime.

Each time, she has changed things, but has never managed to change the ending.

This time, in this life, she hopes that it will be different. So she makes the biggest change of all - she tries to avoid meeting him.

Her soulmate. The love of her life.

Because maybe if they don't meet, she can finally change her destiny.

But fate has other ideas...

I'm Here

When Marielle finds out that a guy she had a crush on in school has passed away, the strange occurrences of the previous week begin to make sense. She suspects that he is trying to give her a message from the other side, and so opens up to communicate with him, She has no idea that by doing so, she will be forming a bond so strong, that life as she knows it will forever be changed.

Nathan assumed that when he died, he would move on, and continue his spiritual journey. But instead he finds himself drawn to a girl that he once knew. The more he watches her, and gets to know her, he realises that he was drawn to her for a reason, and that once he knows what that is, he will be able to change his destiny.

In gratitude for the nourishing vibrational
energy of the trees that have sustained me for
so many years, I have created:

Sacred Tree Spirit

In this dream-like space, you can
receive intergrated therapies, emotional
and core-belief re-programming and
vibrational healing.
You can relax in the mineral spa,
watch life-affirming films in our
imaginarium, attend courses and shop
for handmade gifts.
Or you could just come along for a
drink and a cake to meet like-minded
people.

sacred-tree-spirit.com

designs from a
different planet

madappledesigns
.co.uk

Peace of St🖤ne

9 Swan Court, Monmouth, NP25 3NY

Crystals

Jewellery

Gifts & Homeware

Crystal Therapy Treatments

Reiki Treatments

Hopi Ear Candling

Intuitive Workshops

www.peaceofstone.com

DARKHORIZONSMEDIA

My name is Jason, and I am a Graphic Art Designer and Fine Art Photographer. I create art covers and do promotional photo-shoots for bands all around the globe, and create cover art for print and eBooks. Always ready to take on bigger challenges and adventures, I have recently become an On-set Stills Photographer and Graphic Design Artist for a feature film.

Over the years I have developed my own unique style, and every day I am driven by my passion to express myself through my art. I work closely with my clients to create the look and feel that they want, to best represent their own passions.

You can see my Fine Art Photography online:
facebook.com/mordecaiphotography

You can see my band cover art and graphic art
on my website:
darkhorizonsmedia.com

If you would like to get in touch,
please e-mail me on:
darkhorizonsmedia@gmail.com

This book was published by The Amethyst Angel.

A selection of books bought to publication by The Amethyst Angel.
To view more of our published books visit **theamethystangel.com**

We have a selection of publishing packages available or we can tailor a package to suit each author's individual needs and budget. We also run workshops for groups and individuals on 'How to publish' your own books.

For more information
on Independent publishing
packages and workshops offered
by The Amethyst Angel, please
visit **theamethystangel.com**

Printed in Poland
by Amazon Fulfillment
Poland Sp. z o.o., Wrocław